The Eyes of the Goat

OCCUPATION: THIEF
MANHUNT
THE JURYMAN
SCENT OF DANGER
DANGEROUS SILENCE
KNIFE EDGE
THE GENIAL STRANGER
DOUBLE EXPOSURE
COOL SLEEPS BALABAN
THE LONELY SIDE OF THE RIVER
SALUTE FROM A DEAD MAN
DEATH IS A FRIEND
THE QUIET KILLER
DEAD STRAIGHT
NIGHT BOAT FROM PUERTO VERDA
THE KYLE CONTRACT
SLEEP IS FOR THE RICH
POSTSCRIPT TO A DEAD LETTER
ZALESKI'S PERCENTAGE
RAVEN IN FLIGHT
RAVEN AND THE RATCATCHER
RAVEN AND THE KAMIKAZE
DEEP, DARK AND DEAD
RAVEN SETTLES A SCORE
RAVEN FEATHERS HIS NEST
RAVEN AND THE PAPERHANGERS
THE LAST OF THE BOATRIDERS
RAVEN'S REVENGE
RAVEN'S LONGEST NIGHT
RAVEN'S SHADOW
NOBODY HERE BY THAT NAME
A SAVAGE STATE OF GRACE
BY ANY ILLEGAL MEANS

The Eyes of the Goat

Donald MacKenzie

St. Martin's Press
New York

Library of Congress Cataloging-in-Publication Data

MacKenzie, Donald
    The eyes of the goat / Donald MacKenzie.
      p.   cm.
    ISBN 0-312-09056-0
    I. Title.
    PR9199.3.M325E9   1993
    813'.54—dc20   92-37739
                                        CIP

First published in Great Britain by Macmillan London Limited.

First U.S. Edition: March 1993
10 9 8 7 6 5 4 3 2 1

For the McCreery family, Bob, Jeanette, Richard, Selby and Kate.

The Eyes of the Goat

Chapter One

It was cold in the room with the french windows open. Struan Dunbar blew a stream of cigarette smoke into the chilly March day. There was a NO SMOKING sign propped on the mantelpiece behind him. The Victorian house was on the west side of Kensington Square. A well-fed tom cat stared through the railings of the communal gardens, its tail lashing slowly. Dunbar put his heel on the butt and shut the french windows.

He was fifty-two years old with a rangy build and the deep-set blue eyes of his Ross and Cromarty ancestors. His hair was the colour of salt. He was wearing a dark grey business suit with a white shirt and black shoes. He had left his overcoat with the maid who had let him in. He looked at his watch again. His host was thirty-five minutes late for their meeting.

The drawing room was furnished in period with heavy mahogany pieces. Curtains and chair covers were the same shade of ivory. A cabinet displayed a collection of eighteenth-century musical boxes. Turkish rugs were strewn across the parquet flooring. A Turner watercolour hung on the wall above the fireplace. A number of silver-framed photographs featured his host posed in the company of the famous. Most of the photographs were warmly inscribed to George Brewster.

Dunbar took a seat on the sofa. It was the second time in two weeks that he had been in this house. Since then he had done his homework on Brewster, using one of the embassy computers. Information was stored about

5

prominent businessmen. The program offered little about Brewster's early years. There was a record of his birth in Clapham, London on 18 January, 1926, the only son of a piano tuner. There was no mention of Brewster's schooling or early years. The account of his antecedents jumped forward. After working as an interpreter for UNESCO, he shouldered his way into the entrepreneurial jungle of London. By the time he was sixty Brewster owned a national newspaper, a firm of educational publishers and a stake in European satellite television. He was also on the list of the twenty richest men in the UK with homes in London, Scotland arÍd the Cayman Isles. A confirmed bachelor, he escorted a succession of attractive women and was a staunch supporter of the Liberal Democratic Party.

Dunbar disliked most of what he knew about Brewster. The man's donations to charities were widely publicised, his face and opinions constantly in the public eye. It was Brewster's reputation as an opportunist that had hooked Dunbar's interest.

A paperweight on the table caught Dunbar's eye. The small gold figure represented a rampant goat. He was still looking at it when the door opened.

Brewster came forward behind outstretched hand. 'I'm sorry to keep you waiting. Sit down and make yourself comfortable.'

Brewster was sixty-five years old, bald-headed, with short arms attached to heavy shoulders. A dark, expensively tailored suit disguised the flab round his midriff. He took a folder from a drawer in a side-table and sat down opposite Dunbar. He spoke with a Cockney accent and a Henry Kissinger delivery.

'I know a lot more about you than I did the last time we met.'

'I'd have thought Ned Fletcher would have told you all that you needed to know,' Dunbar said mildly.

Brewster wagged a finger. 'Ned's reliable enough, but

according to him he hasn't seen you in years. I wanted up-to-date information.'

Dunbar took his hand from his chin. 'Ned and I were at university together. After that, we drifted apart the way people do. Then I read about him working for you in Vienna. That's why I asked if he'd give me a letter of introduction.'

'Which he did and I'm glad,' said Brewster. He took a sheet of paper out of the file. 'Why does he think that you wanted to see me?'

Dunbar made a pass in the air with his hand. 'He thinks I'm going to ask for a job, I guess. We didn't go into it. He knew I was just about to retire from the Foreign Service.'

Brewster bent thick bushy eyebrows. 'Ned's a good newspaperman. I wouldn't like to think of him even guessing the truth. When *are* you taking retirement?'

'The end of April.'

'If he ever mentions it,' said Brewster, 'I'll have to say that you didn't come up to scratch.'

Dunbar moved a shoulder. 'Whatever.'

Brewster donned a pair of spectacles and lifted the typewritten sheet. 'I'm not going to bother to read out all this stuff, just the salient points. Let me know if you have a problem with any of it.'

He read in a voice devoid of all feeling.

'Born May 1 1940 in Stratford, Ontario. After attending various schools you enrolled in the University of Toronto. You graduated three years later with a degree in Commerce. Then you were headhunted by the Department of Foreign Affairs and joined the department training scheme. You were posted to Washington a year later. Was that as Trade Counselor?'

'Assistant Trade Counselor,' Dunbar corrected.

Brewster returned to the printed word.

'It says here you were married to Margaret Wakeford, an American citizen. There was a daughter, Catriona. You were posted to Brussels the following year, your

7

wife divorced you three years later. Do you know what happened to her after that?'

'She died seven years ago,' Dunbar answered. Whatever emotions he might have felt then no longer meant anything.

Brewster put the piece of paper back in the file and locked both hands behind his head.

'I understand that your daughter lives with a man called Grattan.'

Blood reddened the back of Dunbar's neck. 'I don't see that my daughter's private life is of any concern to other people.'

'You're asking me to put up a great deal of money. I need to know all I can about you. How do things stand in Prague?'

Dunbar widened his legs and leaned forward. 'I saw my people last night. They're asking half a million dollars US for six computer discs and the codes to go with them. If we decide that we like what we see there are more. The price for these would be negotiable.'

Brewster had the paperweight in his right hand, weighing it. 'What it really amounts to is this. I'm expected to trust your judgement as well as your honesty.'

Dunbar kept a tight grip on himself. 'We've been through this already, Mister Brewster. I *know* the clout that those discs represent. That's why I came to you in the first place. If you want to pull out, so be it.'

'Has anyone ever suggested that you might have a personality problem? A difficulty in communicating?'

'No,' said Dunbar. 'I've been in the Foreign Service for the best part of thirty years. I've always been able to make myself understood very clearly.'

Brewster put the figure of the goat down and viewed it admiringly. Then he raised his head.

'I'll tell you what I've decided to do. I'm putting five hundred thousand dollars in a Swiss account in your name. You can begin to draw on it as from tomorrow.

8

Here's the name of the bank and the person you deal with.'

He passed a card across the table. Dunbar glanced at the name and address and put the card in his wallet.

'Buy the six discs,' Brewster said. 'You speak fluent Czech so you'll know what we're dealing with. If I like what I see, we'll go for the rest.'

'Aren't we forgetting something?' Dunbar said. 'What about my finder's fee?'

'Fifty thousand and expenses. Ten per cent if I go for more. Agreed?'

'Agreed,' said Dunbar.

'Good. There is one thing,' added Brewster. 'I don't want my name mentioned in any of this.'

It was difficult for Dunbar to conceal his impatience. 'I've already explained. We're not breaking the law, Mister Brewster. We're simply acquiring information. And there's nothing that anyone can do about it.'

Brewster had moved to the window and was looking down at the gardens. He turned.

'If there's a risk involved, no matter how marginal, I make it my business to stay out of the firing line. If it ever comes to my ears that my name has been mentioned this whole thing is off.'

'Fine by me.' Dunbar looked at his watch. 'I'd better be off. I'll try to get on a plane for Zurich tonight. If not, first thing in the morning. I'll have time to go to the bank and catch the next flight to Prague. I should have some news for you the day after tomorrow.'

'Then I'll see you,' said Brewster. 'Don't bother phoning. Just be here.'

He opened the door. Dunbar heard it close again before he had reached the stairs. He reclaimed his coat and walked up Kensington High Street into a travel agency. Fifteen minutes later he left with a ticket for Zurich that night.

A cab with its light on slowed for the signals at the bottom of Church Street. Dunbar jumped in quickly.

'Walton Street. I'll tell you where when we get there.'

He had no idea how good his daughter was at her job. It was the first she had had as far as he knew. Her life had taken a predictable course after her mother's death. Catriona spent the life-insurance money travelling. Dunbar had a succession of postcards from places like Goa, Papeete, Paraguay, Malaysia. They exchanged the odd telephone call. She seemed content with the way she lived, but Dunbar knew she had already spent most of her mother's inheritance and would need more than her income to support her current lifestyle.

The cab stopped in front of a boutique with the word BIZARRO inscribed on the window. The shop was closed. He rang the bell at the side. Footsteps descended the stairs and the door opened. Catriona had none of her father's rangy build or colouring. She was small-boned, of medium height with green cat-like eyes and light-brown hair. It was cut in a boyish bob that made her look younger than twenty-seven. Her polo-necked sweater and trousers were black.

She threw her arms round her father and hugged him tightly. 'Papa! What are you doing here in London?'

'Business,' he said.

'Let me have a look at you,' she said, holding him at arm's length. 'You've lost weight. Are you eating properly?'

'I eat when I'm hungry,' he said. Their relationship had suffered since her mother's death. It was good to be with her again. To make up for lost time.

'Well don't just stand there!' she fussed. 'Come on upstairs.'

They climbed, his arm round her waist. There were two open doors on the first floor. On the right was the kitchen. She led him into the sitting room and took his overcoat.

The glass-fronted bookcase dwarfed the low ceiling. One of the shelves held a row of books he had given her, J. M. Barrie, Beatrix Potter, *A Child's History of Canada*.

10

All were in their original dust jackets. Most of the furniture had been her mother's. He recognised the low teak table and chairs, the life-size porcelain cat that grinned in the corner. He nodded across at it as Catriona returned with a tray.

'I see you've still got that goddam thing!' He'd never liked it.

'Don't be unkind. Balthazar's beautiful.'

She put a bottle of Bell's and a glass on the table in front of him.

A picture of Henry Grattan smiled from the mantelpiece. He was thirty-six years old with challenging eyes and a strong, deeply dimpled chin.

Dunbar produced an envelope from his pocket and pushed it across the table.

'Am I drinking alone?'

'It's too early for me,' she said, looking down at the envelope. 'What's this?'

'Open it,' he said.

She hooked a nail under the flap and pulled out the sheaf of hundred-dollar bills. Her lips moved as she counted them silently. She glanced up at her father.

'There's five thousand dollars here, Papa!'

'A belated Christmas present,' he said.

She took a cigarette from his pack and lit it. Her green eyes searched his face. She put the money back in the envelope.

'Have you robbed a bank or something?'

'I don't need to rob banks,' he said, smiling. 'They just hand me the money.'

He showed her the card with the bank address Brewster had given him.

'So?' she demanded.

He put the card back in his pocket. 'I took a long hard look at myself. Fifty-one years old and due for retirement. I decided to better our situation.'

Her cigarette burned unsmoked in the ashtray. 'You'll

11

still have your pension. It's not as though you have any responsibilities.'

'Sure,' he agreed. 'I could live in Florida like the people I've always tried to avoid. Something came up a few weeks ago. If it goes the way I hope, I should have more money than I can spend.'

'What is this? Some sort of scam?' she said suspiciously.

'It isn't a scam,' he said. 'I just thought it was time to feather our nests. Not just mine, yours as well. You've gone your own way since your mother died. I've never been in a position to help you. All that's going to change. You want to buy your own business, then that's what you'll do. And we'll get one thing straight, Catriona. There'll be no strings attached. As long as you're happy that's all I care about.'

They matched looks for a second. Excitement brightened her eyes.

'Can I tell Henry? I don't like keeping secrets from him.'

'There's no need to keep secrets. When are you two getting married?'

'We're not,' she replied. 'I've seen what marriage can do to people. We've lived together for almost two years. We don't *need* to get married.'

He nodded. 'I guess you've got a point there. Is Henry working?'

Her voice was defensive. 'He's sitting in a room with five other people, selling space. He picks names from a list and calls them. He starts at ten in the morning and finishes at seven o'clock at night. He doesn't get a salary, just commission on whatever sales he makes. It's no job for someone like Henry but there is a recession. And at least he's trying.'

'You can change all that if you want,' said Dunbar.

'I've got an idea,' she said enthusiastically. 'Why don't you stay until Henry gets back? We'll take you out to supper.'

He looked at his watch. 'I can't do it, honey. I'm flying

12

to Zurich in a couple of hours and my bag's still at the hotel.'

Her chin lifted. 'Are you telling the truth, Papa. Or is it because you don't want to meet Henry?'

'It's got nothing to do with Henry,' said Dunbar. 'I don't mind who he is. Just as long as he makes you happy. Look, I'll be back in a couple of days. I'll call you from Prague and tell you when.'

She held his overcoat as he donned it.

'I wish you could stay,' she pleaded. 'You'll like Henry, I know you will.'

Dunbar buttoned his coat. 'I can't do it, there's no time. I'm going to be running on rails for the next few hours. But I *will* be back and don't worry. Everything's going to turn out OK.' He kissed her gently. 'And never forget, your father really does love you.'

Catriona accompanied him down the stairs and unfastened the street door. A taxi had just unloaded a few yards away. Dunbar gestured and the cab crawled forward. Catriona clung to her father's hand.

'I'm so glad you came by, Papa. It's been too long and I really do worry about you.'

He suddenly thought of her mother, leaning from a window in Brussels, watching him drive away. He'd returned nine hours later to an empty apartment. Margaret had gone, taking Catriona with her. The next time he saw his daughter was five years later.

He kissed her. 'There's nothing to worry about,' he promised.

Chapter Two

Raven braked, peering through the swishing windscreen wipers, waiting for the woman in front to concede a parking space. Rain had been falling for the last couple of hours. He'd already driven round the block twice.

He was forty-seven years old with grey-blond hair that needed cutting and sharp blue eyes. His wife always said that he had the face of an actor, that he rarely showed what he was really thinking. It was fair comment and it was just as well. Half the time he was just as unsure himself. Years as a policeman had taught him the merit of reflection. He was wearing a dark-blue suit with a chalkstripe and an unaccustomed tie. He looked at the back of the car. His wife had taken the umbrella that usually lay there. He grabbed his trenchcoat and sprinted for the lights of the restaurant.

La Vie en Rose was at the Harrods end of Walton Street. The French couple who ran it were friends of the Ravens. Jean-Pierre Bertrand still cooked in the kitchen, greeting the occasional customer whenever he felt like it. His wife controlled the till, his daughter served drinks at the small bar upstairs. The Ravens ate there at least once a month.

Raven pushed through the curtains into the bar. Paulette Bertrand greeted him with cries of alarm, taking his coat and giving him a towel to dry his face.

Stairs led down to the restaurant. There was nobody else in the bar. He put the towel on the counter.

'Is my wife downstairs?'

The girl's pert face clouded. She gave him a slip of paper. 'She called half an hour ago. She left this number.'

He took the phone to the end of the cord and turned his back. He dialled and lowered his voice.

'What the hell's going on? Have you forgotten what day it is?'

'I haven't forgotten,' said Kirstie. 'Maggie's been drinking again. I just can't leave her like this, John.'

Maggie Sanchez was a one-time model who had lived with a friend of Raven. The man had been killed. Maggie had hit the bottle.

'She's totally out of it,' Kirstie explained. 'The gala performance, ranting and raving. I'm scared that she'll do something foolish.'

'She's been doing that for years,' Raven said tartly.

His wife made a sound of disgust. 'You can be a cold-hearted bastard at times.'

'I know,' he said. 'Can you imagine a man wanting to be with his wife on their wedding anniversary?'

'I'm sorry,' Kirstie said stiffly. 'I thought George was a friend of yours.'

'He was,' said Raven. 'George has been dead for six years. I'm the one who pays for his grave to be tended. Are you going to join me or not?'

He already knew the answer. Maggie Sanchez belonged to the sad sorority of women who blamed their dead lovers for the intense grief in their lives. But Kirstie was loyal.

'I can't,' she said firmly. 'Why don't you have something to eat and come round here?'

'On my wedding anniversary? No,' said Raven. 'You want to play Florence Nightingale, fine. But don't expect me . . . Hello?'

The line had been cut.

Raven put the phone back on the bar. 'Whatever you do, don't get married,' he said.

Madame Bertrand sat at a desk near the foot of the stairs. She was a birdlike woman who wore a shawl winter

15

and summer. The Ravens were one of her favourite couples. He told her that he was eating alone and she clucked her condolences.

The waitresses were French, most of them students. One of them showed him to his table. He ordered an omelette and Perrier water. He ate hurriedly, his mind bent on getting back to the boat. Maybe Maggie would pass out or something. He had no real belief in the thought.

The girl brought his bill and a scribbled note.

It's been a long time, read the message. *We're sitting across the room. Why don't you join us? Henry Grattan.*

The name went straight to Raven's long-term memory bank. The third floor at New Scotland Yard, the cramped quarters of a detective inspector on the Serious Crimes Squad. A call had come through on the hot line. Raven had taken it. A firm of Victoria pawnbrokers said that they were detaining a man who had tried to swindle them out of six thousand pounds. The manager explained what had happened. Raven knew the scam well. It was still used in the provinces. Only a very bold spirit would try it on in the metropolis. The success of the fraud depended on a confident front and a dexterous piece of sleight-of-hand. The thief carried two diamonds, one genuine, the other fake. The settings were identical. The thief chose a busy pawnbroker and claimed that he wanted to pledge a diamond ring. The clerk put the stone under close inspection and made an offer that was always refused. The thief would leave the cubicle, switch the fake ring for the genuine article and return. He'd had second thoughts and would take the offer. It was a matter of chance whether the ploy succeeded.

Raven and his sergeant arrived at the pawnbroker's shop to find the culprit sitting relaxed in the manager's office. He gave his name as Henry Grattan with an address in Bermondsey. The two rings lay side by side on the manager's desk in front of him. Grattan readily admitted his guilt, even joking about his failure. It was his

16

first attempt, he said. He needed more practice. Raven booked him and checked with the CRO. There was no history of any previous arrest. Grattan pleaded not guilty in front of the magistrate. Committed to Knightsbridge Crown Court, he changed his plea to guilty, accepting full blame and responsibility.

Raven knew that there was no way in which a nineteen-year-old would have the means to finance such a fraud. Grattan denied this. It was his own idea, he insisted. Raven had seen too many thieves to believe that a marked sense of honour existed among them. Fear was the one thing that kept their mouths zipped. When the judge asked for Grattan's antecedents, Raven leaned lightly on the man in the dock. The judge sentenced Grattan to a year's imprisonment suspended for twelve months.

Raven eased his way through the crowded tables to where Grattan was standing. The years had been kind to the younger man. He was a touch fatter in the face, making the dimple in his chin appear even more deeply chiselled. He was wearing a well-cut sports jacket, tan slacks and a broad smile. A bottle of Krug peeped from an ice-bucket. A girl with green eyes and a boyish haircut looked up from the table.

Grattan put his hand on her shoulder. 'This is Catriona Dunbar. My old mate Mister Raven, darling.'

She fluttered her fingers, her green eyes slightly out of focus. There was a dead bottle of wine on the side-table.

'Hi!' she said.

Grattan pulled up a chair for Raven. He filled a third glass.

'We're celebrating,' said Grattan.

'That's what I'm supposed to be doing,' said Raven. 'My wife got held up.'

Grattan was clearly pleased with himself. His hand fell to his companion's waist.

'Catriona's old man just laid some money on her.'

'It helps,' said Raven. He lifted his glass. 'Congratulations.'

17

He had no idea what he was doing there but at least he was welcome.

'I heard that you'd left the police,' Grattan said.

Raven nodded. 'That was a long time ago. Do you live around here?'

The question was aimed at Grattan but it was the girl who answered.

'We live a couple of hundred yards away. I manage a boutique called BIZARRO.'

'And what about you?' Raven said to Grattan. 'What are you doing with yourself these days?' In an odd way he was glad to run into the other man. At least he wasn't in jail.

'What am I doing?' Grattan repeated. He put the empty bottle upside down in the ice-bucket. 'At the moment I'm selling space.'

'All that's going to change,' said his girlfriend. 'Henry's got a lot of good ideas.'

'I'm sure,' said Raven. 'Look, I've got to go. Thanks for the drink, Henry. It was good to see you again. Bye-bye, Catriona.'

Grattan was standing now. 'Are you still on that boat?'

'Still there,' Raven said cheerfully. 'Why don't you drop by some time?'

'That would be nice,' said Grattan. 'We'll be in touch anyway.'

Grattan watched Raven to the top of the stairs and turned to Catriona. 'That guy used to be a cop. He nicked me when I was nineteen years old.'

The room was hot. Catriona's hairline was dark with sweat. 'You're putting me on, I hope.'

He shook his head. 'I'm dead serious, Catriona.'

She cupped her chin in her palms and studied his face. 'I thought we were really close,' she said. 'No secrets from one another. You never told me you'd been in prison.'

'I haven't,' he said. 'But I might well have been if it hadn't been for the man you just met.' He gave her his dimple-chinned grin. 'A guy like me is bound to have secrets.'

He called for the bill and placed two fifty-pound notes on the plate. 'Let's get out of here.'

They were in bed half an hour later, pleasantly drunk, the lights out. The headlamps from passing cars chased across the ceiling. Rain lashed the double-glazed windows.

'You're right,' Grattan said sleepily. 'I should have told you before. Your old man isn't going to like it.'

Catriona snuggled closer. 'He isn't like that. He doesn't give a damn as long as we're happy.'

Raven went out to the car. He sat at the wheel, rain obscuring the windscreen. Grattan was still on his mind. Raven was glad to have seen him again, impressed by the girl he was with. Maybe that was what Grattan had always needed. Someone who believed in him. Someone who saw past the façade of the likeable rogue. In the meantime Grattan seemed to have kept out of trouble. Maybe he was trying to buy back a piece of his past. Raven wished them both well. He smiled to himself. His interest was almost proprietorial. They had as much chance as everyone else. And if Raven could help them why not.

By the time Raven reached home, the rain had hardened to sleet. Overhead lamps shone on both sides of the black swollen river. He parked the Ford in the cul-de-sac in front of his houseboat. The flotilla of floating homes came in all shapes and sizes. An upriver paddle-steamer, a couple of Second World War torpedo boats, home-built craft that hadn't slipped moorings in years.

The *Albatross* had once been a brewery barge used to haul grain. The hold had been decked. A cedarwood superstructure covered two-thirds of the boat. The timber was fragrant and durable. Shipwrights had fashioned two bedrooms with a connecting bathroom. There was a kitchen on the port side and a living room that was forty feet long and eighteen in width. Raven had bought the boat soon after he had joined the police.

He crossed the Embankment to a flight of stone steps. He shut the door to the gangway behind him, reminding himself that the lock needed fixing. The barge was moored lengthways, stern facing downriver. It was secured by rope hawsers and chains. Old truck tyres did duty as fenders. He kicked the slush from his shoes, and found the light-switch. An electric motor moved heavy velvet curtains in front of the panoramic windows. His desk, like the much-darned Aubusson carpet, had come from his aunt's home in Suffolk. The chintz-covered couches and armchairs were provincial Ontario. A dividing wall at the end of the long sitting room held shelves with storage cupboards. There was a picture of Kirstie on top of the desk. The pose showed her leaning against the mast of a dinghy. Raven had taken the picture. A notice pinned behind her read DÉFENSE DE MONTER À BORD. Her hair had been much longer then and she was deeply suntanned.

Raven hung his trenchcoat in the corridor and ran a bath. He sat on a chair and pulled a small jewellery box from his pocket. The carved green heart inside was fashioned from emerald matrix. He placed it under his pillow. He took his bath and got into bed. He read for a while, lulled by the swish of the bilge below deck. The door at the foot of the gangway slammed hard. He padded into the sitting room and waited. The deck door opened. His wife stood, wide-eyed over the scarf that protected her mouth. She stripped off her raincoat without speaking.

He followed her into the kitchen. She stood the umbrella in the sink.

She put her head down and shook her honey-blonde hair. 'She's asleep,' she said shortly.

He followed her through to the bedroom. She started undressing.

'I called her doctor. He gave her a shot. She's sleeping.'

He started to say something but she put her hands over her ears and went into the bathroom.

She was out in ten minutes, a towel round her body, scrubbed and smelling of bath oil.

She was thirty-five years old with the body and breasts of a teenager.

She looked at him sorrowfully. 'I guess I'm not going to hear the last of this, am I? Holding a drunken woman's hand while my husband celebrates our wedding anniversary alone in a restaurant.'

'Why don't you get into bed?' he said. 'I'll bring you something hot to drink.'

She was under the covers when he returned with a mug. She cradled the mug with both hands.

'Were there any pretty girls in the restaurant?' she asked.

He got into bed beside her. 'Only one that I noticed and she was with somebody else.'

She finished the milk and put the mug on the bedside table. 'Who was she?'

'It's not the girl,' he said. 'It's the guy she was with. I busted him a long, long time ago. A streetwise kid who'd got himself into trouble. He seems to have straightened himself out. He lives with this girl in Walton Street. Another Canadian, I gather.'

She snuggled under the duvet. 'Let's hope it lasts. I mean the young man going straight.'

'He's not so young any more,' he said. 'Oddly enough, they were celebrating too. I had a glass of champagne with them.'

He reached under his pillow and put the suede box in front of her.

'Happy anniversary, darling.'

She opened the box and gasped. 'It's beautiful,' she said, reverently. 'I didn't even have the chance to pick up your present.'

'I've got enough socks as it is,' he said.

21

She lifted his hand and pressed it against her lips. 'I won't do it again,' she promised.

He grinned. 'You always say that and I always believe you.' He groped for the light-switch. 'You want to read?'

She moved her head on the pillow. 'I just want to be next to you.'

They lay like spoons in the darkness. His knees locked behind hers.

She was still holding the small jewelled heart in her fingers.

Chapter Three

Dunbar found coins for the waiter from room service and pulled the breakfast-trolley into the room. Dunbar's newly pressed suit lay on the bottom shelf. He ate breakfast in front of the window. The Swiss, like the Germans, got off to an early start. The hot rolls came wrapped in napkins, the coffee was Salvadorean. A card from the hotel management invited Dunbar to enjoy his stay with them and presented him with the day's newspapers.

He'd made no phone calls since he arrived the night before. He had no need to telephone ahead and inform the embassy of his movements. The new Assistant Counselor was Hugh Wylie, an amiable British Columbian. Prague was his first posting in Europe. Dunbar gave him the same treatment he gave the rest of the embassy staff. He was always polite but discouraged any attempt at a closer relationship. Seeing his daughter had eased his conscience. He was sure that he was doing the right thing for both of them. He was less certain about Henry Grattan's place in the equation. There was no doubt that he and Catriona were fond of one another. Dunbar's concern was with Grattan's sincerity.

It was twenty past eight Friday morning when Dunbar paid his bill. He entrusted his bag to the concierge and asked for directions. The man smiled. There were more banks than dentists in Zurich, he said with civic pride. Most of them were on or around Bahnhofstrasse, the city's main thoroughfare. Dunbar turned up his coat collar. It was no more than a ten-minute walk to

Stahlbank Verlag. Dunbar glanced at the shops as he passed. Many of them were multi-national with branches in London, Paris, New York and Rome. There was no place for the poor in Zurich.

Dunbar found the Swiss hypocritical in their show of neutrality. They balked at any attempt to make them take sides, refusing to say yes when a no would have been inadmissible. He turned right where a narrow body of water flowed into the lake lower down. The office building on the right was a glittering expanse of glass and steel. The massive bronze entrance doors were shut. Dunbar thumbed a bell. A security guard in the lobby checked Dunbar through the glass. He opened the door.

The lobby was bright with artificial daylight. There were no cigar-stands or newspaper vendors. Just the security guard and a row of elevators. One of them was marked STAHLBANK VERLAG. The express car rose smoothly. Dunbar emerged into a reception area. There was a profusion of cut flowers and house plants. A girl took Dunbar's name and asked him to wait. It was unlike any other bank Dunbar had seen. The room was uncomfortably furnished in Scandinavian style. The windows looked down on a carpark.

A door opened. A short man with a square grey haircut and dark suit came forward. The frames of his spectacles stretched as far as his cheekbones.

'Mister Struan Dunbar?' he queried in English.

'That's right,' said Dunbar.

'You have some identification?'

Dunbar showed his passport. The details on the title page allowed him quick passage through customs and immigration control.

The banker returned Dunbar's passport. 'I am Doktor Halbherr, Mister Dunbar. We have received a credit for five hundred thousand US dollars in your favour.'

Dunbar nodded easily. 'There'll be other payments.'

Halbherr gave him a file-card. Dunbar signed it. The banker's breath emitted a strong smell of cloves. 'As you know we are a private bank. We have no other branches. But we can arrange all financial transactions. I have had a cheque book prepared for you.'

'I don't need it right now,' said Dunbar. 'I'll let you know.'

'Perhaps you would like some cash?'

'That, yes,' said Dunbar. 'I'd like ten thousand US dollars in bills of a thousand.'

Halbherr excused himself. He returned with an envelope. 'Goodbye, Mister Dunbar. We are pleased to have your account.'

Dunbar left the building. Going into the hotel, he stumbled. He was suddenly short of breath and his hands felt cold. He sat on a chair in the lobby and ordered a coffee. The dizziness passed. He asked for a cab.

It was afternoon when Dunbar landed at Ruzyne airport outside Prague. It was snowing. He reclaimed the black VW Polo he had bought the year before, tax-free in Munich. It took forty minutes to cover the twelve miles to the city. The streets looked drab after London and Zurich, the vehicles clapped out and old-fashioned. Civic Forum had done little to better the lot of those who had voted them into power. Most of the shops were poorly stocked. Restaurants closed without warning. The city relied heavily on public transport. The Metro opened early and closed late. Trams scuttled throughout the day and part of the night. The outlying suburbs were served by buses.

He turned the VW towards the south-east corner of Wenceslas Square. The three-storeyed brown stone building he lived in had once been an almshouse. The Canadian government had leased it six years before, converting it into apartments for embassy staff. Hugh Wylie occupied the top apartment, a couple of girls from the chancellery lodged on the first floor, Dunbar on the bottom. Seniority gave him the right to the one-car garage. The Department of Foreign Affairs had sanctioned refurbishment. The front of the building had been sandblasted, window

25

frames made good and repaired. The garage had been provided with a cantilever door activated by a remote-control unit. This was uncommon in Prague. He backed the car in and lowered the door. The caretaker lived in a flat behind the garage. A few steps led into the communal hallway.

There was no mail for Dunbar on the table outside his flat. He let himself in. A padded bench followed the line of the sitting-room wall, a small table in front of it. The furniture was government property. The kitchen contained everything a man living alone would need. A cooker, a freezer and a refrigerator. The shelves of canned food was replenished whenever Dunbar remembered.

He took his bag through to his bedroom. There were two phones on the table. Although one of them was a direct line to the Ambassador's residence Dunbar never used it. The StB, the old state security police, had been disbanded but there was still doubt about the new regime. A Sanyo portable television set stood at the foot of the bed. Dunbar followed the ice hockey games in the winter. He relied on the BBC for a balanced view of world affairs. The only picture on the wall was of Catriona.

Dunbar unpacked his bag, throwing his soiled shirts and underwear through the bathroom door. The woman who cleaned the flat took care of his laundry. He picked up the phone.

A woman's voice answered. 'This is the Canadian Embassy. How may I help you?'

'Struan Dunbar,' he said. 'Put Miss Homolka on the line.'

The girl on the switchboard made the connection.

'I have Miss Homolka on the line for you now, Mister Dunbar.'

'Lada!' he said. 'I'm back. How does my desk look?'

His secretary's English was the result of intensive study, formal but adequate.

26

'There are a couple of urgent letters that need your signature. I've taken care of the rest.'

'You'd better bring them round here,' he said. 'I'm at home. Take a cab.'

Three Czech nationals worked at the embassy, Lada Homolka and two other secretaries. All three had been vetted by the ex-RCMP inspector who was the embassy security officer. Dunbar's association with Lada Homolka had led to his trip to see Brewster.

He moved to the window as a taxi drew up outside. He opened the door to the street. His secretary hurried into the flat. He closed the door again.

She sat down with her legs close together. She was wearing a shapeless tweed coat and a fur hat that looked like an old wet dog. She was thirty years old with pale blue eyes and an anxious face.

'Sit down,' he invited. He took the two letters from her hand and glanced at them briefly. He chose his words carefully. 'You asked me for help, Lada. Why didn't you tell me the truth? Your brother's in jail, not a hospital. Didn't it occur to you that Rotbart would tell me?'

'I was afraid,' she said.

'He's been in jail for over a year.'

She dabbed at her eyes with a handkerchief. 'I did what my brother told me to do, Mister Dunbar. He said that Rotbart would help him to get out of prison.'

'You gave Rotbart my telephone number here?'

She was now weeping openly. He waited until she composed herself. 'Do you know why Rotbart wanted my telephone number?'

'I guessed it had something to do with Petr's job at the factory. Something to do with explosives perhaps. I just don't know.' Her voice was choking with misery.

Dunbar looked at her curiously. 'Are you telling me that's all Petr said?'

She used her handkerchief again. 'I never see him alone. There is always somebody with us. We are not allowed to talk in a foreign language or discuss prison

27

conditions. Petr managed to smuggle a letter out. It was the first time I ever heard of Rotbart. Petr told me to telephone him.'

'What exactly did your brother do at the Semtex factory?'

'He was a research chemist.' She covered her face with her hands.

'You deceived me, Lada,' said Dunbar reproachfully.

'I wish I could take it all back.' She uncovered her face again, her voice still miserable. 'You have always been kind. Have I got you in some sort of trouble?'

Dunbar shook his head. 'No. But I want you to forget about Rotbart. For your brother's sake as well as mine. Is that clear, Lada?'

'Yes,' she whispered. She lifted her head. 'I'd give my life for Petr – I'm all he's got in the world.'

He signed the two letters and pushed them into her handbag. 'I promised to help you and I will. But remember! If you mention a word of my connection with Rotbart to anyone it could lead to disaster. There should be a cab on the corner. I'll see you on Monday.'

He closed the street door behind her, alone in the house again. His neighbours were still at work.

He lifted the phone. 'I have to see you,' he said in Czech. 'Can I come now?'

'You know the address,' said the voice.

Dunbar turned the car right on the one-way street. Traffic was heavy when he reached Bartoskova. Prague's workforce clung to crowded buses and trams. The Volkswagen trundled over railway lines. High powered arc-lamps illuminated acres of repair sheds and coal stacks. A steep slope ahead climbed to a huddle of houses. A few cars were parked outside a chapel. Dunbar manoeuvred the Volkswagen as close as he could to the other cars. He walked a few yards to the house on the opposite side of the clearing. The door opened as he approached. He followed Rotbart into a room that was empty except for a couple of folding chairs.

Milan Rotbart was in his fifties with a thin, hard face and slate-coloured eyes. He wore a black leather jacket and gumboots.

He pushed one of the chairs at Dunbar and sat on the other. There was a paper bag on the floor by his feet. No matter what the rest of his face did his eyes remained watchful.

Dunbar pulled the envelope from his pocket. 'Ten thousand dollars – a mark of good faith. The rest of the money's in Zurich.'

Rotbart counted it. He put the envelope in his pocket and pushed the paper bag across with his foot.

'You get the codes when the balance is paid.'

Dunbar opened the paper bag. The six computer discs looked like any others to him except for the markings.

'You understand that I have to be sure what I'm buying,' he said. 'I need proof that the information on the discs is the same as you promised.'

Rotbart clicked his tongue on his teeth. 'I have already told you. I give you the proof when I have the money. We keep our word too, you know.'

'OK,' said Dunbar. 'I'll call the bank tomorrow. There is just one more thing. I'm talking about Lada Homolka. She's worried about her brother.'

Rotbart's eyes were as cold as a snake's. 'You can leave him to us.'

'From now on I want Lada kept out of this business,' said Dunbar. 'Just do what you promised for her.'

Rotbart showed his teeth briefly. 'I see no difficulty with that. She has served her purpose.'

Dunbar pushed his chair back. 'You said there was more information for sale.'

Rotbart yawned and stretched. 'There is. How long will it take to get the money?'

'I should have it here by tomorrow,' said Dunbar.

'I'll call you then,' said Rotbart.

The evening chapelgoers were leaving as Dunbar hurried across to the Volkswagen. Warmly dressed children were running down the slope, yelling. Dunbar fastened his seatbelt and started the engine. He drove back over the railway lines and rejoined the highway. The lights of the oncoming traffic blinded him, momentarily. Pain exploded in his chest. He lurched sideways, still held in the seatbelt. His last living act was to reach for the ignition key. The Volkswagen veered left towards the truck coming in the opposite direction. The noise of the crash echoed in the darkness beyond the grass verge.

Chapter Four

Catriona Dunbar put the pressure cooker to soak in the kitchen sink. Her attempt at fish stew had been a disaster. Even Grattan had suggested as much. She carried the coffee into the sitting room. He was still on the couch, feet up, the computer discs on the table beside him. He was wearing jeans and an open-necked shirt. A plume of dark hair was sticking up at the back of his head. It was twenty minutes past eight.

Catriona looked at herself in the mirror. Her dove-grey dress increased her pallor. Her eyes were hollow and strained. She had not slept properly since hearing of her father's death. The news had come from the embassy in Prague. At first she refused to believe it. The man's voice had been calm and commiserative. It was understood that Catriona was her father's sole living relative. Unless she objected, the Department proposed shipping Dunbar's body back to Toronto for burial. Still shocked, she agreed, unable to face the thought of a church full of strangers. The funeral had taken place without her. Dunbar's desk had been cleared, his personal effects returned to Macdonald House. The computer discs had been in the suitcase that Catriona collected.

The discs seemed to fascinate Grattan. He had taken all six to a friend, a computer programmer for British Telecom. The verdict was swift and unequivocal. There was no way of viewing the information stored on the discs without the entry codes.

Catriona poured two cups of coffee. Grattan reached

out lazily, lighting her cigarette. He returned to his original position on the couch and aimed his voice at a spot on the ceiling.

'OK. Let's see what we've got here. Question one, do you think that your father was bullshitting you?'

'I've never seen him so calm and sure of himself. He meant every word that he said.'

He switched his gaze from the ceiling and focused on Catriona. 'You father turns up here unannounced, lays five thousand dollars on you and says that you're both going to be rich. Next thing we hear, he's dead from a heart attack. And this is a guy who passed a physical only two months before.'

'So what?' she demanded. 'That's why people with heart attacks *go*. There aren't any dress rehearsals.'

He shook his head at her slowly. 'There you are then. What we do is take the computer discs to Prague and start asking questions.'

'You're out of your mind,' she said impatiently. 'My father didn't have any friends in Prague. And you don't speak Czech.'

'You're forgetting your pa's secretary, Lada Homolka. As far as we know she was the last person to see your father alive. She left his flat a couple of hours before his death. I want to ask her some questions, like where your father went that night. She must know where it was.'

The gas log fire hissed in the silence. Catriona was unconvinced.

'We could go together,' he urged. 'We've got the money your father gave you.'

She was losing the battle and knew it. 'I can't *do* that,' she objected. 'I've got the boutique to run.'

'Then I'll go myself,' he said calmly. He sat up straight and took both her hands.

His diction was clear. 'I want you to have what is rightfully yours, darling. I don't intend to sit on my butt and watch everything slide away from you.'

She found herself being swayed by his enthusiasm. His

suggestions might not be sensible but he always managed to make them sound plausible.

'The whole thing seems crazy to me,' she said, freeing her hands. 'How long would you go for?'

He lifted his shoulders. 'Long enough to talk to Lada Homolka. I should be back in a matter of days. Three or four at the most.'

She drew a deep breath of surrender. 'I worry about you.'

'You mean you don't trust me?' he said.

'I didn't *say* that,' she insisted. 'I never trusted anyone more in my life. It still doesn't stop me from worrying.'

'But there's no need,' he wheedled. 'The Czechs are a civilised people. Asking a few questions is all that I'm going to be doing. If people can't or don't want to answer, I'll be on the next plane back to London. Look at you!' he said, pointing a finger at the mirror. 'You don't sleep, you don't eat. Knowing the truth, whatever it is, would at least put your mind at rest.'

She turned away from the mirror. 'Know something? You haven't said one word about me not going to Canada for Papa's funeral.'

'That's because you didn't ask me,' he replied. 'I *know* what you've been through, Catriona. Think of it this way, the funeral was a mark of respect, a tribute. There's nothing your being there would have added to the respect people showed him. Don't be so hard on yourself.'

She was strangely relieved. He had a way of coaxing her out of depression, of stilling her fears. She picked up the empty coffee cups. 'If you really want to go to Prague, there's nothing I can do to stop you. Just come back in one piece, that's all I care about.'

She carried the tray into the kitchen. The sitting-room lights were out when she went back. She followed Grattan up to the bedroom.

It had been snowing in Prague since early morning. Grattan was drinking coffee downstairs in the restaurant. It was after nine. He had eaten here the night before, surrounded by Japanese wearing spectacles and namebadges. They ate with their heads close to their food, shovelling it in with chopsticks. Memory of the meal persisted in Grattan's stomach. He went upstairs to his room. There were clean sheets on the bed, the towels had been changed in the bathroom.

He sat on a chair by the window and called Catriona.

Hearing his voice she went straight for the jugular. 'What happened? You were supposed to call me last night.'

'The flight was delayed,' he said. 'Then it took time to find somewhere to stay.'

'Where are you?' she said tightly.

'The Gambrinus Hotel. It's something out of another world. It's got to be a hundred years old at least. I've got a bathroom the size of the flat.'

Her voice had the tartness of sarcasm. 'Really? Well, your computer friend called just after you'd left.'

'What did he want?'

'We didn't get that far,' she replied. 'You've got some very weird friends.'

'What's that supposed to mean?'

'Well,' she drawled, 'as soon as he knew that you weren't there he wanted to come here and talk. The exact words were "I'll be round in five." '

Grattan laughed. 'You don't want to pay any attention to Joss. He just fancies himself as a ladies' man. I hope you didn't tell him where I'd gone.'

'I hung up on him,' she said.

'I'll have a word with him later,' said Grattan.

'You'll do no such thing,' snapped Catriona. 'You're an endangered species and I want you preserved. What's it like there in Prague?'

He stared through the heavy curtains. Flurries of snow sailed in front of the windowpanes.

'It's drab,' he said. 'Everything's the same shade of grey. The streets, the buildings and the people. And

34

the hotel's full of Japanese grinning and bowing at one another. I miss you, Catriona.'

Her voice softened. 'I miss you too, darling. Have you called the embassy yet?'

'I haven't had time. I only just surfaced.'

'Well, don't get yourself into trouble.'

He closed his eyes. Since meeting Raven she seemed to think he was some sort of tearaway. The truth was he got off by pitting his wits against others. What the headmaster at Borough Street secondary had called 'a perverse wish to indulge in self-destructive fantasy'.

Catriona's voice claimed his attention. 'You can charm birds from the trees when you feel like it, Henry. Just be nice to those people at the embassy. Remember, my father worked there.'

'I'll be respectful. I'll call you as soon as I've got some news.' He smacked his lips at the mouthpiece and put the phone down.

It had been too early for him to shave. He went into the stately bathroom. The make-up mirror was backlit for close inspection. There was a shelf of bottles bearing Hungarian labels. It was a pity Catriona's father hadn't died there instead of Prague. Budapest was supposed to be a fun city. He scraped his face clean and put on his shirt again. He was travelling light, with no more than a change of clothes, his business suit and a black silk tie brought out of respect for Dunbar. His mind dwelt on the best way of approaching this Lada Homolka. One thing stuck in his memory. The computer discs had been found on Dunbar's body. And Lada Homolka was the last person known to have seen him.

He took his camel-hair coat from the wardrobe and checked his money. He had a thousand dollars that Catriona had given him. Some crowns he had bought at the airport. The girl in the travel agency had been adamant. The Czech currency laws were strict. You could get busted changing money on the black market. The girl had added another tip. It was wise to carry your passport

35

with you. The computer discs were still in the brown paper bag that had come from Macdonald House. He'd carried them through two sets of customs without any problems. He put the bag in his jacket pocket, his camel-hair coat over his suit. He picked up the phone again and asked for the Canadian Embassy.

A girl answered.

'I'd like to speak to Miss Lada Homolka,' he said. 'My name is Henry Grattan.'

'I'm afraid that's not possible, sir. Miss Homolka's on leave.'

'Can you tell me when she'll be back?'

'I have no idea, sir.'

'Well, can you give me her home number?'

'We're not allowed to divulge this sort of information.'

Grattan turned on the charm. 'Look, I'm only in Prague for a couple of days and this is important. Is there anyone else I could talk to?'

'One moment, please.'

A man's voice came on the line. 'Mister Grattan? This is Hugh Wylie. I understand you're asking for Miss Homolka?'

'That's right,' said Grattan. 'I believe she was Struan Dunbar's secretary. His daughter's a friend of mine.'

'What exactly do you want from Miss Homolka?'

Grattan detected an edge in the other man's manner. 'It's difficult to explain on the phone,' said Grattan. 'Is there any chance of me talking to you personally? It wouldn't take long.'

'It'll have to be quick,' said Wylie. 'I have a lunch appointment at one and it's almost that now. Where are you staying?'

'The Gambrinus Hotel.'

'OK, that's not too far away. You'd better come over.'

Grattan took the computer discs out of his pocket and locked them away in his overnight bag. There was no point in taking unnecessary risks.

He went downstairs to the lobby. The doorman summoned a cab. The driver turned his head. '*Wohin, bitte?*'

'The Canadian Embassy,' said Grattan. It was the third time in a few hours that someone had assumed he was German.

It had been dark when he drove from the airport the night before. This was a different experience. They went past an endless series of one-way streets and pedestrian malls. Buildings under repair were covered in scaffolding. This city would be a nightmare for a stranger to drive in. After the initial exchange, the driver was silent. They crossed a bridge over a wide sweep of river. The traffic moved slowly under the snow. There was no sign of aggression, no leaning on horn buttons. Foot passengers muffled in winter clothing walked carefully, avoiding the slush sprayed from passing vehicles.

The driver was threading a needle of narrow streets and climbing. Grattan recognised the skyline from the posters he had seen in the travel agency. A complex of palaces clustered around the castle. The gothic spires of the cathedral showed beyond. The driver swung the cab to the kerb and jerked his thumb.

The embassy stood solid behind iron railings. Snow was beginning to build on the fountain and courtyard. Grattan rang the bell marked VISITORS. A security guard answered the summons. He peered through the railings.

'I've got an appointment with Mister Wylie,' said Grattan.

The security guard ushered him into a large hallway hung with a picture of Queen Elizabeth.

The man knocked on a door and motioned Grattan inside.

The room was furnished like a library with well-stocked bookshelves, black leather club chairs and a wide desk with three telephones.

A tall man rose behind the desk. He had cropped sandy hair, spectacles, and was built like a baseball player. He

37

was wearing a button-down white shirt with a narrow tie and blue slacks.

'Sit down,' he invited. He put the tips of his fingers together. 'I take it you're not a Canadian citizen, Mister Grattan?'

'I'm a Brit, a Cockney in fact.' In an era of East End whizkids and barrow-boy millionaires he had learned to make capital from his origins.

Wylie smiled distantly. 'So what do you want to see me about, Mister Grattan?'

Grattan dragged the ashtray nearer. He closed an eye against the rising smoke from his cigarette.

'You must have taken over from poor old Struan, right?'

Wylie nodded. 'His death was a great shock to all of us here.'

'What I have to say is a delicate matter,' said Grattan.

'Rest assured that anything you say here is privileged,' said Wylie.

'That's what I'd hoped,' said Grattan. A man like this he could handle. 'Struan was worried about his daughter's future, frankly. He was coming up for retirement, no money except his pension. What he did have was some highly specialised knowledge. Are you with me?'

'Go ahead,' said Wylie.

'He wanted to put this knowledge to use. He made me a proposition. He seemed to see himself as a sort of bridge between the West and the developing countries. He said there were good prospects for someone with the kind of contacts he had. I just left his daughter in London. She's a very close friend of mine.'

Wylie hitched up his spectacles. 'Dunbar had every right to do whatever he wanted,' he said mildly. 'But I don't see what that's got to do with me. Or for that matter Lada Homolka.'

'Please be patient,' said Grattan. 'I'm not a rich man, Mister Wylie, but I do have access to venture capital. A deal is something I understand. Struan and I talked this

38

thing back and forth but he never put all his cards on the table. There were reasons, he said. People who had to be taken care of first. What he needed was some up-front money.'

Wylie's interest revived. 'So you found it for him. Is that what you're saying?'

Grattan spread his hand in resignation. 'He promised to give it back in seven days' time. Next thing I know, I get a phone call from his daughter. She told me that Struan had died from a heart attack. The money I lent him wasn't mine, Mister Wylie.'

Wylie frowned. 'Every single item found on his body was checked by me personally. His effects were returned to his daughter in London. As far as I can recall there was no money to speak of.'

'I know that,' said Grattan. 'But there were some computer discs. His daughter showed them to me. I wondered if they could have something to do with the deal he was supposed to be setting up.'

'I've no idea,' replied Wylie. 'Dunbar's stuff was kicking around here for almost a week. We had to get clearance from the Czech police before we could send it on. There may have been these discs that you're talking about. I just can't remember.'

'There was a list of the stuff that was sent to London. Lada Homolka's name was on it.'

'It would be,' said Wylie. 'She's the one who typed all the correspondence.' He looked at his watch.

Grattan stubbed out his cigarette. His voice was casual. 'I wondered if Dunbar might have talked to her about the discs.'

Wylie laughed. 'You've got to be kidding! We seem to be talking about two different guys here. Look. I worked with Dunbar for over a year, lived in the same building, I never got past his front door. Apart from official business I had no idea what he did with his time. He was a very private person. Where are these discs anyway?'

'They're in London,' said Grattan.

39

'OK,' said Wylie. 'I'm trying to put myself in your position. The girl on the switchboard was perfectly right. There are regulations against divulging information about embassy staff. And that includes the Czech employees. I'll tell you what I'll do. I'm going to bend the rules in this case. I'll call Miss Homolka and tell her what you've told me. If she wants to get in touch with you, well and good. It's the best I can do.'

It was still snowing outside. Grattan walked for ten minutes before he found a cab. He remembered reading that Prague lay north of Winnipeg. The knowledge impressed him for some curious reason.

'The Gambrinus Hotel,' he said firmly in English.

He stared through the window. The discs meant nothing to Wylie, he was sure of it. Only time would tell if they meant anything to Lada Homolka.

The cab stopped outside the hotel. He went up to his room and lay on the bed for a while, the phone within reaching distance. It was eight o'clock when he went down to eat. The message over the PA system caught him halfway across the lobby.

'A telephone call for Mister Grattan. Will Mister Grattan please go to the nearest telephone?'

Grattan went to the reception desk. 'Henry Grattan here.'

The woman's voice sounded hesitant. 'I'm Lada Homolka. Mister Wylie from the Canadian Embassy just called. He said that you wanted to talk to me.'

'I do,' he said. 'It's very important. I can meet you anywhere you like, Miss Homolka. Just say the word and I'll be there.'

'Your hotel isn't far away. About twenty minutes' ride. I can come there if you like.'

'I'll be waiting,' he promised. 'I'll tell the doorman.'

It was half an hour before she arrived. He was on his feet immediately.

'Miss Homolka?'

She took off her gloves and placed her hand in his

40

briefly. She was nothing like the woman he'd expected. Colourless was the first word he thought of. And meek. Like a novice in her first years at convent. She had a thin, unattractive face. A shapeless tweed coat and ratty fur hat did nothing to flatter her appearance.

'It's going to be hard to find a place where we can talk in private,' he said. 'Would you mind coming to my room?'

Her muscles were tense as he steered her across to the lift. She avoided his eyes as the car rose. He walked her along the empty corridor and opened his door.

He placed the small couch with its back to the window.

'Don't be nervous,' he said. 'I'm not going to eat you.'

She loosened her coat and removed her hat. She made a brave attempt at a smile.

'You'll have to forgive me. I haven't been feeling well.'

She sat down and took a cigarette from the package he offered. She held it between thumb and forefinger, taking small nervous puffs without inhaling. She was clearly unused to smoking.

Sitting beside her he laid an arm along the top of the couch. 'Did Wylie say why I wanted to see you?'

'Yes. He said you wanted to ask me about poor Mister Dunbar.'

'I do,' he said. 'How long did you work for him?'

'Four years and two months.'

He had the feeling that she could have given him the precise time down to the minute.

'You must have been close,' he suggested. His fingers were near the back of her hair. He was careful not to make contact.

'He was the best friend I ever had, apart from my brother,' she said. 'A man with a heart.'

'He was a friend of mine, too,' Grattan said, nodding slowly. 'You know that he left a daughter?'

'Catriona. He often talked about her.'

Grattan stared at his shoes for a moment and looked up again. 'Did Struan ever talk about his plans for her?'

41

She made a face and put out her cigarette. 'No. We all knew he was retiring. The impression I got was that he intended to stay in Europe. To be near his daughter, I suppose.'

Grattan changed course. 'I saw him when he was in London. He thought very highly of you.'

Her lips started to tremble. 'He was my only hope.'

She burst into tears unexpectedly, hiding her face in her hands. She pulled away on the couch and looked at him.

'I'm in such terrible trouble. And there's no one I can talk to. Nobody.'

'I'm here,' he said gently.

'Such terrible trouble,' she repeated. 'I'll lose my job if the embassy knows about it.'

'Look,' he said, 'you're not the only one who's in trouble. The only reason I'm here is to see *you*, not the goddam embassy. It seems to me that we both need help. Dunbar was my friend too. If you tell me what's bothering you, maybe I could take his place.'

She dabbed at her eyes with a handkerchief and sat up resolutely.

'I just can't go on like this any longer. My brother's in prison. Mister Dunbar was going to help get him out.'

'Why did he go to prison?'

'They never told him. He was a research chemist in the Semtex factory. The police arrived during the night and just took him away.'

The signals were loud in Grattan's brain. 'When was that?'

'More than a year ago. They used to let me see him but I can't even do that any more. They stopped me. Petr managed to smuggle a letter out. There was this telephone number in it, someone called Rotbart. I showed the letter to Mister Dunbar. He got in touch with the man.'

'Now listen,' Grattan said very carefully. 'You've just

42

helped me more than you know. Now it's my turn to do something for you. Have we got a deal or not?'

She thought for a while before answering. 'I trust you.'

'Good,' he said smiling. 'I lent Struan some money, Lada. Money that wasn't mine. Those computer discs that were sent to London. How much do you know about those?'

The question obviously surprised her. 'Nothing at all. All I did was type the correspondence. I'd never even *seen* the discs.'

'I believe you,' said Grattan. 'Can you remember the telephone number in your brother's letter?'

She took an address book from her bag and showed him an entry.

'I write all my numbers backwards. It's a habit. My parents were very strict.'

'OK,' he said. 'Struan is dead, right? There's nothing that you or I can do to change it. He never had the chance to do all the things he wanted. Maybe we can finish the job for him. I'm going to make you a solemn promise, young lady. Whatever Struan was doing to help your brother, I'll do the same.'

He put the phone in her lap. 'I want you to call that number,' he said tapping the address book. 'Tell Rotbart you're with a business associate of Dunbar. You can give him my name. That's no problem. Just say that I'm prepared to do business. Make sure you say that. I'm prepared to do business.'

She spoke to the girl on the switchboard, speaking in Czech, and waited for the connection to be made.

Grattan had no idea what was said but heard his name mentioned.

She cradled the phone and shivered. 'Even his voice scares me. He's sending a car for you at six o'clock.'

'Did he mention the discs?'

'Not a word. But he seemed to know who you were.'

'How do you mean?' he said, frowning.

'It was the way he spoke. As though he was expecting you.'

She excused herself and went into the bathroom. Five minutes went by. She came out, her face washed and her hair brushed. She sat on the couch again.

He spoke on a hunch. 'Does Rotbart work for Semtex security?'

She moved her head from side to side. 'I don't know. But I do know that he frightens me.'

Looking at her, he had an idea that he'd taken Dunbar's place as far as she was concerned. The thought heightened his natural bravado.

'Let me take care of Rotbart.'

'I'm worried about my job,' she said.

'Don't,' he assured her. 'Nobody's going to know a thing. This is between you and me, Lada.'

She scribbled a telephone number and gave it to him. 'I won't be back at work for another three days. Call me at home tomorrow.'

'Why not tonight?'

'Because I won't be there.' She picked up her hat and her bag. 'It is better that you do not come down with me, please. Goodbye, Mister Grattan, I'll be expecting your call.'

The door closed behind her. He unlocked his overnight bag and took out the computer discs. He sealed the envelope and took it downstairs. Lada had gone. Grattan strolled across to Reception and placed the envelope on the counter. 'Will you put this in the safe, please?'

The clerk made out a receipt. 'The safe's open between six a.m. and midnight, sir. You can retrieve your deposit any time between those hours.'

Grattan returned to his room. He pulled a chair to the window and stood on it. Then he pinned the receipt to the outside of a curtain. There was no chance of it being seen from the street. It was twenty minutes to six. He lit a cigarette and waited.

The phone rang. 'Reception. Your car is here, sir.'

The Skoda station-wagon standing under the lights out-side was painted a metallic shade of grey. Its exhaust blew petrol fumes into the falling snow. The back of the vehicle was littered with sacks and gardening tools. It seemed natural to get in front with the driver. The man was wearing a black leather jacket and a woollen cap pulled low over narrow-set eyes the colour of wet slates. He took a quick glance at the rear-view mirror.

'You speak Czech?' he asked in English.

'Not a word,' said Grattan.

The man continued to stare at him for a few seconds before engaging the gears. Grattan understood what Lada Homolka meant.

Their route took them away from the lights of the city centre, the driver constantly checking the scene behind in his mirror. He drove fast but defensively, making no move to overtake unless it was safe. The traffic was thin now, just a few red-and-green trams. They skirted a long brick wall and turned into a carpark in front of a cheerless apartment building. The snow was beginning to build on the asphalt.

The man cut his headlamps and sidelights leaving a small glow in the roof of the vehicle.

'My name is Rotbart,' he said.

It was a moment before Grattan's eyes adjusted to the sudden plunge into comparative darkness.

Rotbart spoke English with ease and a trace of a Cock-ney accent.

'Where do you live in London?'

'Does it matter?' said Grattan. They were a couple of hundred yards from the road. It seemed like a mile.

Rotbart settled his back on the door. 'Everything mat-ters where you are concerned, Mister Grattan.'

'OK,' said Grattan. 'I live just off Fulham Road, Walton Street.'

Rotbart removed his cap and smoothed his hair. 'Mister Dunbar had a daughter who lived there.'

'That's right,' Grattan said cheerfully. 'Dunbar was an associate of mine. That's why I'm here.'

'Who gave you my name?'

'Come on, now,' Grattan said, smiling. 'I was with Lada Homolka when she called you. I've no time to play games, Mister Rotbart, if that *is* your name.'

'It's my name,' said Rotbart.

'OK. I've known Dunbar for a number of years. Three weeks ago he came to me with a proposition. I liked the sound of it. So I put up some money. Dunbar moved the money to Switzerland. That's the last that I heard of it.'

'How much was it?'

'Enough,' Grattan said shortly. He had to be careful here.

Rotbart's voice grated. 'What were you supposed to be buying?'

'I wasn't,' said Grattan. 'It was Dunbar who was doing the buying.'

Rotbart sucked in his cheeks. 'You've got a saying in English, "A pig in a poke". Is that what you do, buy a pig in a poke? Is that the way you do business?'

Grattan found himself floundering. 'Look. Dunbar was more than a business associate. He was a friend. Of course I knew what he was buying! He was buying confidential information, confidential information that was stored on computer discs, six of them to be precise. You see, I inherited Dunbar's assets as well as his debts. And if you're going to ask me where the discs are at this moment, the answer is London.'

Rotbart's grin exposed a row of stained teeth. 'Your friend didn't keep his part of the bargain.'

'People who die rarely do keep bargains,' said Grattan. The story was coming along nicely. 'I'm offering you the same deal as he did.'

'The price for the codes has changed,' said Rotbart. 'We have been under a lot of pressure. We want a million dollars.'

'That's a great deal of money.'

46

A car stopped thirty yards away. Rotbart screwed his head round and watched the man extinguish his lights and go into the apartment building. He turned to face Grattan again.

'Do you have that much money?'

'I can find it,' said Grattan. 'But this time I'd have to be sure what I'm buying. A transcript at least.'

'That could be arranged,' said Rotbart. 'You went to the Canadian Embassy this morning. What was that for?'

'I'll tell you what it was for,' said Grattan. 'Their people are the ones who sent Dunbar's effects back to London. I wanted to know how much importance they attached to the computer discs. The guy couldn't even remember them. I had another reason for going as well. I wanted to get in touch with Lada Homolka. And that's exactly what I did.'

Rotbart's tone changed. 'A million US dollars,' he said. 'How long will it take you to find it?'

'A day or two, a week at most,' said Grattan, thinking ahead. This was even better than he expected. There must be someone in London who would want what he'd got. Dunbar had to have had a buyer.

'Does that mean that you would be going back to England?'

'No,' said Grattan. The truth was that he had to get out as fast as he could. He had things to do. Meanwhile he had to keep Rotbart contented. 'It's a matter of making some telephone calls. The bank will arrange the transfer.'

Rotbart turned the ignition key. 'I think you and I can do business. I'll call your hotel tomorrow. Will that be all right?'

'Fine,' said Grattan. 'You'd better leave it until after six.'

Rotbart listened to the sound of the engine. 'Do you like girls?' he asked suddenly.

'Yes,' said Grattan. 'As long as they're five feet eight tall with green eyes.'

'Tomorrow night we will celebrate,' said Rotbart. 'I will introduce you to a girl with green eyes.'

Rotbart drove out of the carpark and turned left instead of right as Grattan expected. They were heading back towards the river. Grattan recognised none of it.

'It's a terrible feeling not to know where you're going,' he said after a while. 'Where the hell *am* I going?'

'The Gambrinus Hotel,' said Rotbart. 'It is not wise to follow the same route always.'

He stopped the station-wagon on the corner of Wenceslas Square. 'I will be in touch. Good night, Mister Grattan.'

Grattan retrieved his key from Reception. His first thought was the computer discs. He climbed on the chair. His fingers closed on the small piece of paper pinned to the outside of the curtain. He was resolved to get the discs and himself out of Prague as soon as he could. There was no chance of getting hold of the codes without the money. The shit would hit the fan when Rotbart realised that there *was* no money. Why hadn't he said that he'd have to go back to England to raise it? The answer of course was Rotbart's suspicious manner. He'd lost the deal once with Dunbar. Grattan was Dunbar's replacement. Rotbart didn't want to lose him too.

The bar downstairs was crowded with Japanese back from their excursions. Some of them had found female company. Grattan crossed the lobby. He exchanged the ticket for the brown envelope containing the computer discs.

'I need to send this by registered post. It's going to the UK.'

He printed the address. CATRIONA DUNBAR 399 WALTON STREET LONDON SW3 UNITED KINGDOM. He completed the customs form. CONTENTS: COMPUTER SOFTWARE. NO COMMERCIAL VALUE.

He pushed the package across the counter and watched the clerk use the scales.

'Have you any idea when that will get there?' asked Grattan.

The clerk affixed stamps to the small package. 'It'll be on its way before midnight. It should be in England within forty-eight hours.'

Grattan sat down at a writing-desk across the lobby. He wrote a short note on a piece of hotel stationery and enclosed the registered mail receipt in the envelope. He stamped it and dropped it in the postbox. He went to his room and consulted the list of return flights. He called the airport and gave the details on his ticket. His flight for the following morning was confirmed within minutes.

He asked for Catriona's number in London.

'It's me,' he told her. 'I'll be back tomorrow. About eleven thirty your time at Heathrow.' He heard the sound of the television set in the background. She was up in the bedroom.

'Tomorrow?' she repeated.

He grinned at the mirror. 'What's the matter? You haven't got someone there, perchance?'

'Don't be ridiculous,' she said. 'What happened?'

'A lot. I can't talk too much on the phone but I think we're in business. I'm talking about the software. I'll see you tomorrow. Byeee!'

He looked at his watch and went downstairs to the restaurant. There was no fish on the menu. He ate venison.

It was almost ten o'clock when he went back to his room. It had been a long day and he needed a good night's rest. He was lying on top of the bed when the telephone rang.

The woman's voice sounded middle-aged. She spoke in English. 'I must apologise for calling you at this hour, Mister Grattan. I'm a friend of Mister Wylie at the Canadian Embassy. The Trade Counselor. I believe you met him?'

He leaned back on the pillow. 'What can I do for you?'

49

'We've been trying to get hold of you all afternoon. At least, Mister Wylie has.'

'I had to go out. What does he want?'

'I have no idea, sir. I found this message on my answering machine. Would I find out if you were still in Prague. My name is Helena Markova.'

The name meant nothing to him. 'Do you work at the embassy too, Mrs Markova?'

'No, I don't. I'm just a friend of Hugh's.'

'And you don't know what he wants to see me about?'

'No,' she replied. 'But he did say it was important. He wanted to see you sometime tomorrow if that was possible.'

'No chance, I'm afraid,' said Grattan. 'I'm flying back to London early tomorrow morning.'

'Oh dear,' she said quietly. 'Hugh had the idea that you were going to be in Prague for the next few days.'

'There was a change of plan. Do you know where Wylie is at this moment?'

'He's in the country, having supper with some people. I don't even know their name. But he'll be calling me some time tonight and I'll give him your message. What time does your plane leave, Mister Grattan?'

'Early,' he answered. 'I have to be at the airport by nine thirty.'

Her voice was regretful. 'That's too bad. Ah well. In that case there's nothing to be done. I'll explain things to Hugh. And I'm sorry to have bothered you.'

He read for a while. The phone rang again as he started to run a bath. He hurried into the bedroom. It was Helena Markova again.

'Mister Grattan? Hugh just rang from the country. I told him that I'd managed to get hold of you. He was very concerned to hear that you're leaving Prague. He says he has information that you ought to know about. Is there any chance of your meeting him later tonight?'

Grattan looked at his watch. 'It's twenty past ten,' he objected.

'I know. He's cutting his supper short and driving straight to his flat. Do you know where it is? It's in the same building as Mister Dunbar's old flat.'

'I know where it is,' he said quickly. He had the address in his book. 'I'll leave right away,' he promised.

'I'll tell Hugh,' she said. 'I think you might be taking good news back to London.'

Grattan collected his overcoat. Hugh Wylie assumed fresh importance. It was Wylie who had cleared Dunbar's desk at the embassy. Who knew what he might have found? Maybe he was the new player, about to sit down at the table.

The cabdriver seemed engaged on some obstacle course that ended on sagging springs. He gestured at the short one-way street ahead, unable or unwilling to go any further. Grattan pushed money into his hand. The taxi drove off. Scabs of snow were forming on windowsills. The houses seemed to lean sideways. The short street was only partially lit. Grattan scanned the numbers over the doors. There was no logical progression. Numbers jumped from one side of the street to the other. Coloured plaques on the walls confused the issue. Suddenly he saw the house that he wanted. There was a tangerine-coloured door. A slit of light showed behind a shuttered window. The rest of the house was in darkness. There were three bells on the panel. Grattan pressed the top one. The echo chased the noise through the house.

The street door opened. The step was six inches high. The light from the hallway shone down into Grattan's eyes. He raised his head, taking in first a pair of stout walking shoes. A sensible coat covered the woman's body. Spectacles gave her the look of a district nurse.

'Come in,' she fussed, closing the door. He recognised the voice. It was Helena Markova.

Someone upstairs was hoovering. There was a table with flowers on the right of the hallway. The door

51

opposite bore a small plate with Struan Dunbar's name on it.

She turned the handle. 'Go on in,' she invited. 'Hugh's waiting for you.'

The room was completely bare of furniture. The carpet had been removed. Patches on walls showed where pictures had hung. The kitchen door was ajar, revealing bare boards and a disconnected refrigerator. The light Grattan had seen from outside came from a lamp near the shuttered window. It was cold in the flat; the heating was off.

Something moved in the bedroom. Grattan turned quickly.

'Mister Wylie?'

Rotbart stepped into the room holding a thirty-eight calibre pistol fitted with a silencer. He grinned. 'I wanted to make sure that you caught your flight.'

It was difficult for Grattan to force the words from his mouth.

'My partner called. He wants me back in England immediately.'

The lie died to the sound of the hoover upstairs. Rotbart's eyes showed no mercy. 'You're a cheat and a liar. Here's a message to your friends back in London.'

He swung the gun in an arc that ended between Grattan's left ear and his temple. The effect was instantaneous. Grattan dropped to his knees like a stone through water. He held the pose for a second and pitched forward. Rotbart bent over and lifted his eyelid.

Rotbart opened the street door and whistled. A car crept forward, Helena Markova peering through the frantically working windscreen wipers. A man wearing a lumberjacket sat next to her. He jumped out and helped Rotbart drag Grattan into the back of the car. Snow continued to fall on the empty street. Rotbart threw a blanket over Grattan's recumbent body and planted both feet on it.

Markova drove into the network of narrow streets and swung left towards the river. Visibility was poor. The car stopped behind some scaffolding. Markova cut the headlamps. Rotbart searched Grattan's pockets, leaving the money and passport. There was nothing else.

He placed the silencer-muzzle in the middle of Grattan's forehead and fired three shots in rapid succession. The reports made no more noise than a sheep coughing. Grattan's head erupted in a welter of blood, brains and bone-splinters.

Rotbart wrapped the rug round the body and dragged it behind a hoarding. There was a storm-grating a few feet away. He dropped the gun through the bars and took his place in the car. Helena Markova sought his eyes in the rear-view mirror. Her voice was uncertain.

'I have seen people killed but I have never been a party to murder before.'

The man beside her grunted. 'None of us do what we want any more. It's survival that counts.'

Rotbart removed his gloves. 'It had to be done. These people must learn who they're dealing with.'

The man in front looked across at the scaffolding. 'What about the house keys?'

'I'll give them back to Homolka,' Rotbart said grimly. 'She's in no position to talk. And remember, none of this ever happened.'

Chapter Five

It was eight o'clock in the evening. Catriona Dunbar was on the phone in the sitting room. She was talking to a clerk in the Czech Air Lines office. It was the fourth time in an hour that she had contacted them.

'The name is Henry Grattan,' she repeated wearily, 'He was supposed to be coming from Prague this morning and he hasn't arrived. I've told you all this before. I don't think you're being very helpful.'

'We are doing our best, madam. What flight was your friend booked on?'

She supplied the particulars and heard a rustle of papers.

'People do miss flights,' said the clerk. 'You'd be surprised at the number of no-shows we get in the course of a day. Do you happen to know where he was staying in London?'

'He lives here,' she snapped. 'We both live here. It's a private house.'

'And the name of the hotel in Prague?'

'Hotel Gambrinus,' she replied. 'I'd have thought it would be a simple matter to look through a passenger list.'

'I already have,' said the clerk. 'There's a reservation for a Henry Grattan but he did not check in at the airport.'

'I don't *believe* this,' she cried. 'He wouldn't just not turn up. I talked to him yesterday night.'

'I'm very sorry,' the clerk said. 'But there's literally

54

nothing more I can do. I suggest that you try the hotel in Prague, madam.'

International Enquiries supplied the Gambrinus telephone number. A woman answered in Czech.

'Don't you speak English?' Catriona asked.

'A little.'

Catriona enunciated slowly and clearly. 'I need to talk to Mister Henry Grattan. He's staying in your hotel.'

'Not here,' the woman said curtly. 'Gone away.'

It was a couple of seconds before Catriona understood that the line had been disconnected. She cleared the remains of her solitary meal, wondering what might have happened. It would be like Henry to reroute at the very last moment without even bothering to tell her. She left the street door unbolted and climbed the stairs again. The idea of reporting her lover a missing person conjured up a vision of bored faces and sly innuendos. And what could they do in any case? This was London, not Prague.

She undressed and climbed into the king-size bed. She was no longer used to sleeping alone. She watched television for an hour or so, zapping from one channel to another. Her eyes kept straying to the travel clock on the small table. Time crept by. It was well after midnight before she dropped off. The alarm woke her promptly. She hurried downstairs and collected the post. There was nothing from Grattan. Her indignation increased. How *dare* he treat her like this!

It was nine thirty by the time she had made the bed and finished breakfast. She dressed in a dark-blue skirt and business-like shirt blouse. It was cold and grey when she opened the shop below.

The first person through the door was a man holding his hat in his hand. He looked round the shop uncertainly. 'Miss Catriona Dunbar?'

'That's me,' she said cheerfully. He looked at her like a VAT inspector. She tried to remember where she had put the records.

'I'm a police officer, miss,' he said, showing her a

55

warrant card. 'Detective Sergeant Armstrong, Chelsea police station. Do you know a Mister Henry Grattan?'

She could see the police car parked fifteen yards away. 'He lives upstairs,' she said. 'We both live upstairs.'

'I think you'd better sit down, miss,' he said, pushing a chair in her direction.

She grasped both sides of the chair and lowered herself very slowly.

The policeman glanced at his notebook. 'Mister Grattan was visiting Prague. Is that correct, miss?'

'That's right,' she agreed. 'My father worked at the Canadian Embassy there. Mister Grattan went over to deal with some business matters. Why?'

He rubbed the side of his jaw. 'I'm afraid I've got bad news, miss. Mister Grattan's body was found by the Prague police early yesterday morning. He'd been murdered.'

She rejected the thought completely. 'That's impossible! There must be some sort of mistake. Henry had no enemies there. Or anywhere else come to that.'

His eyes were compassionate. 'I'm afraid it's true, miss. The police found his passport. Staff at the hotel identified him.'

She took her fingers away from her mouth. 'But how can that be?' she demanded.

He shook his head. 'We don't have anything more as yet.'

'I want his body back here,' she said. 'I want him buried in England.'

His voice was regretful. 'I'm afraid that's a matter for the Czech authorities. I know how you feel, miss.'

'*Do* you,' she said, blinking the tears back. 'First my father, now this,' she said bitterly.

A woman was about to come in from the street. The policeman closed the door on her. 'Have you got a solicitor, miss?'

The question enraged her. She found herself shouting.

'No I do *not* have a solicitor! If you want to know the truth I've got nobody now.'

'How about a friend? Someone who could stay here for a couple of days. You shouldn't be alone here you know. I could arrange for a social worker to come round if you like.'

She felt the blood leave her face as she rose. 'I'll tell you what I'd like,' she said. 'I'd like you to leave right now.'

He clapped his hat on his head, his face concerned. 'It's not easy to do this sort of thing, it always upsets me. But it's part of the job. If you think I can be of any help, call me at Chelsea police station. There's my card.'

She watched him as far as the waiting police car. Her only feeling was a deep sense of loneliness. She closed the boutique and went up to her bedroom. She opened the wardrobe. Grattan's clothes hung in mothproofed containers. His shoes stood in a neat row beneath. He had taken no more than a couple of shirts and a change of underwear. She closed her eyes briefly. And those *bloody* computer discs! If it hadn't been for them he would still be alive. She opened a drawer in the dressing-table. The rest of the money her father had given her was still in her jewel case. She closed the drawer with a sense of guilt, as though she had in some way doubted him. She drew the curtains and threw herself down on the bed in the darkness. Her body began to shake and she wept, hugging her grief to her breast.

It was after six when she woke. She washed her face and mouth and went downstairs to the sitting room. Her lips moved as she placed Grattan's picture face down on the mantelpiece, unable to meet his smiling gaze. She found the telephone number and dialled. A man's voice replied. 'Three four nine, John Raven speaking.'

It was as though she was reading aloud from a script. 'This is Catriona Dunbar, Mister Raven. I don't know if you remember me. I met you with Henry Grattan a couple of weeks ago.'

Recognition was warm in his voice. 'Of course I remember! *La Vie en Rose*. You were celebrating something or other. How are you both?'

'Henry's dead. Murdered. His body was found in Prague yesterday. A policeman came with the news this morning.'

'Jesus!' he said. His voice sharpened. 'Where are you speaking from?'

'I'm at home,' she said dully. 'I don't know what to do, Mister Raven.'

'You get yourself in a cab and come here,' he said quickly. 'Do you know where I live?'

She read the address from the book in front of her. 'The *Albatross*, Chelsea Embankment.'

'That's right. Tell the driver to turn right at the bottom of Oakley Street. The boat's painted white. You can't miss it. I'll be waiting at the top of the steps. OK?'

'OK,' she whispered.

The cab dropped her off quarter of an hour later. Raven stood at the top of some steps. He was taller than she remembered, dressed in a baggy sweater and jeans. His shaggy grey hair needed cutting. He held her close for a second and hurried her down the steps. The line of boats wallowed in the stiff north-east wind. Spray blew as they crossed the deck to the door in the superstructure. It was warm inside the long sitting room. Panoramic windows followed the line of the hull. Raven took her coat and pushed her into a chintz-covered armchair.

'Kirstie!' he called.

A woman in a black lycra catsuit and scuffed ballet shoes came into the room. Her honey-hued hair was tied with a tennis bandeau.

Raven made the introductions. 'This is Catriona Dunbar. My wife Kirstie. Catriona needs a drink, honey.'

His wife sank on to the couch. 'I think we all need a drink. Make mine a Bloody Mary.'

There was a picture of her on the desk near the bowl

of freesias. It showed her leaning against the mast of a sailing-dinghy.

Raven busied himself at the drinks cupboard. Catriona's hand was trembling as she took her glass. He sat down beside her.

'Relax,' he urged. 'You're with friends here.'

Tears started to roll down her cheeks. She dabbed at her eyes with her handkerchief. 'I shouldn't be doing this to you,' she said miserably. 'I just didn't know who to go to.'

Kirstie came to her feet briskly, brushing the cigarette ash from her lap. 'Would you two like to be alone?'

'There's no need for that,' said Raven.

Kirstie shrugged, smiling at Raven. She turned to Catriona.

'You came to the right place, honey. Ladies in distress are my husband's speciality.'

She disappeared in the direction of the bedrooms. Something scuttled across the deck, blown by a gust of wind. Catriona tensed. Raven took both her wrists, forcing her to look at him.

'Take your time,' he soothed. She spoke in a monotone for the next ten minutes about Henry and her father. She stopped suddenly, overcome by a fresh wave of emotion. 'I can't believe that Henry's dead!' she cried. 'I mean, why? What harm did he ever do to anyone?'

'That's what we're going to find out,' said Raven, releasing her wrists. 'What about that card the policeman gave you?'

She opened her handbag and produced it. Raven picked up the phone and dialled. He put the phone down again. 'He's gone off duty.'

Kirstie came into the room again wearing a dark-blue raincoat, her blonde hair pushed into a black velvet beret. 'I have to go out,' she announced, smiling brightly. 'Goodbye, Miss Dunbar. I'm sure John will take care of you.'

Catriona lifted her head. 'I should never have come here,' she said quietly. 'Do you think I should go?'

'Of course not!' said Raven. 'Let me fill you in about Kirstie. I was still on the force when we started living together. I don't know if you have any idea what a cop's life is like, Catriona. There's no privacy. The phone rings and you get up and do your job. That's the way things are. Kirstie always knew this but she didn't like it. When I left the police she thought things would change. So did a lot of other people. It didn't work out that way.'

She put her glass down very carefully. 'I no longer have any shame,' she said. 'I'm begging you, please help me.'

He sat down on the couch beside her.

'Of course I'll help. I'll do whatever I can. God knows you need it. The first thing we have to do is get things in some kind of perspective. It shouldn't be too hard to find out what happened. I still have contacts. Getting the Czechs to return his body might not be as easy. It may help if I go to Prague myself.'

A wave of relief swept over her.

'I've still got the dollars my father left me.'

He was on his feet, swaying with the movement of the boat.

'It isn't a question of money. In a case like this it's who you know that matters.'

She shook her head, her voice bitter. 'I can't even think of anyone. I don't have any friends.'

He pointed a finger at her. 'That's nonsense. Look, you'd better start thinking positively. OK, whose idea was it that Henry should take these computer discs with him to Prague?'

She thought for a moment. 'I guess it was both of us, really. Papa had seemed so sure of himself when he came to see me. He seemed to know exactly what he was doing. For the first time in his life he'd be able to help me, he said. Just a few more days.' Her voice wavered again. 'Then he died. The discs were among his belongings. Henry was sure they had something to do with the deal

Papa had talked about. When this friend of Henry's told him the discs were in code, Henry was sure of it.'

'He could be right,' Raven said. 'The first thing is to find out where the discs *are*. How many times did Henry call you from Prague?'

'Twice,' she replied. 'The first was to say he was seeing the new Trade Counselor at the Canadian Embassy. The last time was the night before he was killed. We didn't talk for long. He said he couldn't explain on the phone. He'd be back in the morning. He just never got on the plane.'

Raven picked up her coat. 'I'm going to put you in a cab and send you home, young lady. Is there anyone you could stay with for a couple of days? What about the woman who owns the boutique?'

'She's in Barbados. Look, don't worry about me, Mister Raven. There's no need. I won't do anything stupid. I promise.'

The wind blew hard as they climbed the steps to the Embankment. Her face looked young and defenceless in the light from the overhead lamp. It was a few minutes before a cab stopped. Raven handed her into it.

'I'll know more in the morning,' he promised. 'I'll call you.'

Back on the boat, he slumped in his favourite chair, a fresh drink in his hand. His mind ran less on Catriona Dunbar than on Grattan. The South Londoner seemed to have died as he lived, flamboyantly.

It was after nine when Kirstie returned. She threw her coat and beret on the couch and looked round the room.

'Where's our guest?'

'I sent her home,' he said. 'You didn't exactly make her feel welcome.'

She put on an air of surprise. '*Me?*'

'Don't give me that,' he said irritably. 'The woman came here for help, in desperate trouble. And you treat her like a piece of shit.'

61

She plumped the cushions where Catriona had been sitting and took her place.

'I had things on my mind,' she said calmly.

'Like what?' he demanded sarcastically. 'Maggie, a forty-year old bimbo with a drink problem. It's about time she got herself another crutch to lean on.'

She put one arm behind her head and looked at him. 'What's happening?'

Her manner stung him. 'I'm going to Prague's what's happening,' he said calmly.

She smiled. 'And that girl's going with you, of course. Look, I live with you, John. I know every trick in your hand. You don't need an excuse to climb on your charger. You were there the moment that girl called you.'

'She's not coming with me,' he said. 'Is it too much to expect you to understand? A man I knew has been murdered, for crissakes. I want to know how and I want to know why. If it turns out to be just another statistic, some foreigner mugged in a bar, that's one thing. But it could be more than that. The two deaths just might be connected.'

'What two deaths are we talking about?'

'Henry and Catriona's father.'

'Oh God, I had no idea.' Kirstie was about to say more but Raven interrupted. 'Why don't you come with me? You're Canadian.'

The fine skin creased near her eyes. 'What's that got to do with it?'

'Dunbar was Canadian. You can help me a lot.' He offered a peacemaking grin. 'Keeping me out of trouble, for one thing.'

She made a moue of derision. 'The odds against that are enormous. Let's get this straight. Are you seriously asking me to go to Prague with you?'

'I *need* you,' he pressed. 'You can take a camera with you. It's a beautiful city by all accounts, untouched by the war.'

She cocked her head. 'That's the nicest thing you've

said to me in a long time. I'm beginning to love you again. When are we going?'

'As soon as I get the answers to a couple of questions,' he said.

Her face bore a look of reluctant admiration. 'You don't change, do you?'

'No,' he agreed. 'I don't change, any more than you do.'

Raven used the phone in the sitting room. Kirstie was still asleep.

'At a quarter to eight in the morning,' shrilled O'Callaghan, 'it could only be you. What do you want?'

'A little civility wouldn't come amiss,' Raven said tartly. 'Why don't you hear what I've got to say before you go into hysterics. Someone I know got himself killed in Prague. A guy called Henry Grattan. I busted him back in the Seventies.'

O'Callaghan's voice was weary. 'I'm in the middle of breakfast, John. Can't this wait?'

'No, it can't wait,' said Raven. 'I don't have the time to hang around in your office all day. This is urgent. Grattan's girlfriend is out of her mind with anxiety. She lost her father last month and now this. She's asked me to go to Prague and find out what happened.'

The lawyer emptied his mouth. 'If the man's dead, she knows what happened. What does she want, a death certificate?'

'Forget the flip patter,' said Raven. 'This is your old chum speaking. Show the compassionate side of your nature, the man who refuses to work for the Crown Prosecution Service.'

'Hold on a minute!' There was the sound of a door being closed, then the lawyer was back. 'Go ahead.'

'That friend of yours,' Raven said. 'The one who works in the Foreign Office. What was his name again?'

'Michael Sheffield. What about him?' The lawyer's voice was suspicious.

'I'm going to Prague tomorrow morning and I don't speak one word of Czech. Catriona Dunbar wants Grattan's body brought back to England. I thought Sheffield might know how I should go about making the arrangements.'

'I can give you the answer to that,' said the lawyer. 'It's no. Sheffield's got a sensitive job. Why would he want to be involved in something like this, for God's sake?'

'Because you'll talk to him nicely,' said Raven. 'You owe me that much at least. Tell him I'm an old chum engaged on an errand of mercy. I don't give a damn what you tell him. Just a few minutes of his valuable time is all I want. Now will you do it or not?'

'Does Kirstie know about this?'

'She's coming with me,' Raven said blandly.

'Then I hope she knows what she's doing. OK, I'll give Sheffield a bell.'

'When?' Raven persisted.

'As soon as you get off the bloody line. I'll call you back.'

Raven replaced the phone, smiling. O'Callaghan's role model was that of a cynical, hard-nosed lawyer. The reality was the opposite. O'Callaghan's courtroom aggression concealed a pussycat who defended no-hopers with the same zeal as his more prosperous clients. The one thing he abhorred was violence. Raven loved the man.

He peeped in on Kirstie. She still huddled under the duvet, a pillow pulled over her head. He disconnected the bedside phone and padded back into the sitting room. Gulls wheeled under a cheerless sky. The rumble of morning traffic had increased along the Embankment. The phone came to life in his lap.

'This is the last time I do something like this,' said the lawyer. 'I've just talked to Sheffield. I don't know how much he can do but he'll see you at five o'clock. Do you know Locatelli's wine bar in Fulham Road?'

64

'I know where it is,' said Raven. The bar was a hangout for estate agents and secretaries. Raven had never put foot in it.

'Be on time,' said the lawyer. 'Sheffield's a busy man. And no crap about an errand of mercy. I've told him all about you.'

Kirstie came into the sitting room in her nightgown.

'Who was that?' she asked, stretching her arms.

'A friend of Patrick's,' said Raven. 'He works in the Foreign Office. He's going to give me a few tips about Prague.'

She yawned. 'What time are you seeing him?'

'Five o'clock,' he replied. 'I'll get the tickets this morning. What are you going to do with yourself all day?'

She looked through the windows and shivered. 'What I'd like to do is go straight back to bed. I'll have to tell my agent I'll be away for a couple of days just in case. And I'm having lunch with Maureen O'Callaghan.'

'Well, don't forget the packing,' he said.

She looked at the clock and gasped. 'I've got a hair appointment at ten. Why didn't you wake me?'

'You looked too sweet,' he replied.

She made one of her quick changes and was gone by the time he came out of the bathroom. He pulled on his jeans and a bomber-jacket. Kirstie had reconnected the bedroom telephone. It rang again.

Catriona Dunbar sounded excited. 'You won't believe this, John. The postman has just delivered a registered package from Prague. You know what's inside? My father's computer discs. And there's a letter from Henry. Should I tell the police?'

'Tell no one,' he said. 'Just stay where you are. I'm on my way over.'

The car keys had gone from the dressing-table. Raven called a cab. Catriona was standing outside the boutique, wearing a green suit that matched her eyes. She hurried him up to the first floor. The first thing Raven noticed was a framed picture of Grattan on the mantelpiece. The glass bore traces of lipstick. Catriona opened a drawer in the bookcase and placed a registered envelope and an airmail letter on the table in front of Raven.

He studied the two postmarks and tipped out the contents. The discs were roughly the size of a music-tape but much thinner. Someone had marked the covers with a ballpoint pen, the letters ST, and a string of digits. He opened the airmail letter. There was a receipt for the registered package inside with a scrawled note bearing a telephone number. Lada Homolka Tel: 264803 (Embassy).

He put the letter and tapes back in the large envelope. 'Are you sure this is Henry's handwriting?'

'Positive.' Her eyes watched his every move.

'I'll take care of this for the moment,' he said, tapping the envelope. 'You said your father showed you a card with the name of the bank in Zurich. Can you remember it?'

She moved her head quickly and reached for her handbag. 'I put it in my diary. Stahlbank,' she read. 'Bleicherweg Zurich 1.'

'Is there anything else in your dairy? Stuff that you wouldn't want other people to see?'

Her look was surprised. 'No. It's not that kind of diary. Just things that I want to remember.'

'Well, keep it out of sight,' he counselled. 'The bank may not know that your father is dead. A whole lot of things could happen. Your father may have had a numbered account. We're going to have to get hold of a lawyer who specialises in these matters. And he will need proof. For instance, your birth certificate and your father's. Can you get these, Catriona?'

'I've got them upstairs,' she said. 'My parents' marriage certificate and Papa's passport. There may be other things. I just haven't had the heart to go through it all.'

'Well, do it,' he said. 'We're going to need everything we can get our hands on. And don't worry about the

66

lawyer, Catriona. I'll take care of that. Sit down for a minute.'

They faced one another across the table. Her eyes filled with fresh anxiety.

'I want you to listen to me very carefully,' said Raven. 'Kirstie and I are flying to Prague in the morning. We'll try to stay at the same hotel as Henry did, the Gambrinus. I'll let you know if we have to find somewhere else. In the meantime, I want you to be brave and trust me. Do you think you can do that?'

She nodded.

'And talk to no one about your father or Henry. If anyone mentions them, no matter who it is, tell them you'd sooner not talk at the moment. They'll understand. Do you promise?'

She took his hand and held it against her cheek. 'I'll never forget what you're doing for me, never.'

'You will,' he said cheerfully. 'We might even laugh about it.' He placed both hands on his knees and cranked himself up. 'I have to go now, and don't forget. Not a word to anyone.'

'I promise,' she said.

Raven's next stop was at the Czech Air Lines offices. He left with two tickets for the following morning. The return halves were undated. The clerk confirmed their booking at the Gambrinus Hotel.

Raven's bank was near Knightsbridge Green. He took one of the discs from the envelope and scribbled Lada Homolka's telephone number on the back of his cheque-book. He sealed the registered envelope and gave it to a cashier.

'I'd like to leave this in the bank for a couple of weeks,' he said. He gave his account number and left.

It was a couple of minutes to five when he walked into the wine bar. The place was more or less what he expected. A mural of the Bay of Naples, fishing nets, table lamps fashioned from empty Chianti bottles. Apart from the girl behind the bar there was only one customer. A man sitting alone near the window. Raven walked over.

'Are you Michael Sheffield?'

The man took a good look at Raven. 'And you must be Raven. Take a chair.'

Sheffield was on the right side of forty with a full head of well-brushed brown hair. He had the clear eyes and skin tone of a man who kept himself in good condition. A deep cleft in his upper lip gave him a slightly sardonic look. He was wearing a dark overcoat with a velvet collar. A bowler hat and neatly furled umbrella lay on the seat next to him.

He pushed the bottle of Perrier water aside. 'Patrick told me about your problem,' he said, 'I tried to reach you at home. I'm afraid that there isn't much I can say that will help you.'

'Why's that?' asked Raven.

Sheffield fingered the tip of an ear and took a quick look at the bar. The girl was polishing glasses. Sheffield lowered his voice.

'I made a few enquiries into the matter. Patrick didn't say that your friend had a criminal record. It put me in a somewhat embarrassing position.'

Raven looked at him. 'I don't believe this,' he said. 'Did Patrick tell you that I was a policeman myself?'

'Yes, he did,' Sheffield said smoothly. 'It seems that you were the arresting officer in Grattan's case.'

Raven spoke very clearly. 'That was seventeen years ago. Grattan was a British citizen holding a valid passport. I thought the Foreign Office was supposed to take care of people like that.'

'We do in normal circumstances. This is an entirely different kettle of fish. For one thing the Prague Criminal Police are in charge of the case. There's nothing HM Government can do until they finish their investigations. I'm sorry.'

A sense of outrage thickened Raven's tongue. 'How about a letter of introduction to the embassy?'

'Out of the question,' said Sheffield. 'This business has caused enough trouble as it is. Nor is it clear what your friend was doing in Prague in the first place. I can tell you this much in confidence. The security services could be involved.'

Raven's fingers closed on the disc in his jacket pocket. 'That's ridiculous!'

Sheffield felt in his coat and passed some newspaper clippings across the table. 'No one can stop you going to Prague, Mister Raven. But things have changed under the new regime. It would be worth your while to glance through these papers. I'd say your best course is to leave your address at the embassy. Let them know where you're staying and wait until they get in touch with you. They'll let you know when the police release your friend's body. In the meantime, you can start making arrangements for its return.'

He picked up his hat and umbrella and left some money on the counter. Raven watched him get into a cab. He picked up the sheaf of newspaper clippings. SCORPION'S NEST! read one headline. SECRET POLICE QUIZ STUDENT LEADERS. VELVET REVOLUTION UNDER THREAT. There was a slim brochure printed on glossy paper. He put the newspaper clippings inside the brochure and stuffed it into his pocket.

The streetlamps came on as he neared the boat. Kirstie was in the bedroom. His overnight bag lay open on a chair. Kirstie had packed it. She was filling her own Gucci bag with clothing. He threw the newspaper clippings and the disc on top of his shirts and fastened the straps.

'How did it go?' she said, looking over her shoulder.

'I got the tickets,' he said. He put them on the dressing-table with his passport. 'We've got a room at the Gambrinus Hotel.'

'I didn't mean that,' she said. 'I'm talking about Patrick's friend.'

'Just a waste of time,' said Raven. 'One of those typical stuffed shirts from the Foreign Office. He gave me a six-minute audience and some newspaper clippings. I need a drink.'

'I'll join you,' she said. She followed him into the sitting room and closed the curtains. They collapsed on the couch together.

'I popped in on Catriona Dunbar this morning,' he said casually.

She poked at the ice in her Bloody Mary. 'Oh really? How was she?'

'A lot better,' he said, treading carefully. 'She had had a good night's sleep for one thing. She'd been going through her father's papers again. You know, stuff that she'll need for the bank in Zurich. I'm going to get the name of a lawyer from Patrick. Someone who deals with that kind of thing. What did Maureen have to say?'

She emptied her glass. 'Not a lot.' She touched the back of her head. 'Do you like my hair?'

'Terrific,' he said. It looked the same to him as it usually did.

She turned on the television. 'Was Catriona glad that we're going to Prague?'

'I guess so,' he said. 'She's finding it hard to come to terms with what's happened. Poor woman.'

'Poor woman indeed,' she said. Suddenly she laughed. 'Your *face!*' she cried.

He took a quick glance at himself in the mirror. 'What's wrong with it?'

'It's the look you put on when you're trying to hide something from me.'

'*Me?*' he blustered. 'Don't be absurd. Why do you make these sort of accusations?'

'Because I live with you,' she said. 'I can hear your hair growing. And there's definitely something you're trying to hide.'

He grinned sheepishly. 'You're a bloody witch. You're right, of course. Catriona Dunbar called this morning. Apparently the last thing Grattan did before he died was send her father's computer discs back to her. That's why she asked me to go round and see her.' He was ready and willing to change the subject.

Kirstie had other ideas. 'Is that what you put in your bag just now?'

'That's right, among other things.' he admitted. 'People are going to be asking what Grattan was doing in Prague in the first place. That's one of the things Sheffield brought up.' He steered clear of any mention of security services. 'Look, I'm supposed to be a friend of Grattan's. I've got to have something to show.'

'*Show?*' she repeated. 'You don't even know what is on the discs. It could be anything.'

'You don't understand,' he said. 'I've got to have some sort of justification.'

'That's something you're never short of,' she answered. 'You'll be a cop to the end of your days, my darling. Sniffing and snuffling after a few lousy computer discs. You just could end up with egg all over your little face.'

'Never mind my goddam face,' he said stubbornly. 'I know what I'm doing.' It didn't matter what was on the discs. What mattered was that they were the reason for Grattan being in Prague. He'd do better not to remind her of it.

He turned off the television set. 'We've got an early start in the morning, Kirstie. Why don't we have something to eat and watch TV in bed?'

Chapter Six

The pre-flight formalities took longer than usual. Security checks were even more comprehensive. A customs officer pulled Raven out of the line of passengers and asked him to open his bag. Kirstie stood a few yards away watching apprehensively. The computer disc was lying on top of Raven's clean shirts. He had made no attempt to conceal it. As Kirstie had said earlier, if anyone asked what it was, Raven would be pushed to supply an answer. The officer's cotton-gloved fingers probed beneath Raven's underwear. He closed the bag and waved Raven on.

Their seats were at the rear of the plane. Kirstie sat by the window. Raven took the seat by the aisle. He needed to stretch his long legs occasionally. They were both travelling light. Kirstie had no more than the jeans and tank top she wore under her Burberry, and a black dress for evenings. Raven had on his dark flannel trousers and blazer. The air hostess passed down the aisle, distributing newspapers in Czech and English. Raven had heard the seven o'clock news on the radio. Kirstie was reading a copy of *Vogue*. Most of the other passengers were British businessmen.

There was a surge of power and the plane was airborne. A few minutes passed and the NO SMOKING signs were extinguished. Raven picked up the booklet that Sheffield had given him. He leafed through the pages at random. Graphs demonstrated the movement of commerce between the UK and Czechoslovakia. The articles were

written in technical language. Raven continued to turn
the pages. The next page took his eye.

FORCE FOUR HAVEL'S WILD CARD?

Elected president by popular acclaim in 1989, Vaclav
Havel was re-elected by parliament just one year
later. In creating his new government he found himself with enormous power to appoint senior minis-
ters. The initial result of what Havel once described
as 'the velvet revolution' was disheartening. Civic
Forum supporters protested against the election of
Communists to the Federal Assembly. Critics
claimed that 'old faces that had been around for
decades' were reappearing. Reforms were being
blocked at all levels. Havel supporters called for the
dismissal from government of all old *nomenklatura*
officials. Bygone scandals were resurrected, the
Communist Party's involvement in unauthorised and
illegal sales of explosives to Iran and Libya. Reference was made to undercover deals with Western
industrialists.

Havel seized the opportunity to create Force Four
in a charismatic and typical approach to the problem.
Force Four began tracking down officers of the old
StB, the state secret police force. Force Four, or FF
as it came to be known, owes its name to the number
of men and women it employs. There were four
hundred of these. None had been trained in conventional police work. Each agent was chosen by Havel
personally. Their ranks are understood to include
soldiers, actors and actresses, forest rangers,
teachers, a pastor of the Moravian Church and the
director of a clinic for handicapped children. FF
agents have two things in common, a fierce and abid-
ing love of their country and a strong belief in democ-
racy.

Founded in September 1990, Force Four has no
conventionally structured hierarchy. Policy decisions

73

are made pragmatically. All agents have the right to request and obtain aid from conventional police forces and security units. They are responsible to Havel alone. Agents are understood to pursue their ordinary occupations when not engaged on a mission. Most of the funding for FF is known to come from emigré Czechs, including various Hollywood personalities and two world class tennis players.

Rumours abound about the exploits of Force Four but one thing is certain. Life for supporters of the old regime has been increasingly difficult. Westerners seeking to do business in Czechoslovakia may never knowingly set eyes on an FF agent but they will never be far from their field of influence.

'Take a look at that,' he said, giving her the article to read.

She scanned it and shrugged. 'What about it?'

He put the pamphlet back in his pocket. 'It seems like a great idea – I wonder no one's ever thought of it before. Come to that, we could do with something like that in England.'

'You're crazy,' she said and went back to her magazine.

They landed ten minutes early. Raven put his arm round his wife as they walked into the arrival hall. It was a lot less sinister than Raven had thought it would be. Passport and customs control were carried out by friendly officials with a reasonable command of English. The only point they insisted on was that foreign currency should be exchanged at banks or approved outlets. Any deviation from this rule could result in a fine or even imprisonment. The first in the line of taxis waiting outside was an ancient but well-maintained Mercedes. The driver was a middle-aged woman with gold canine teeth and a black woollen cap. Raven gave her the name of the Gambrinus Hotel. There was little to see for the first few miles. Conifer trees sheathed in snow, expanses of frozen water and a few roadside shrines. Raven put his hand on Kirstie's. He knew how much first impressions mattered to her.

'It'll be better,' he promised.

The scene changed as they neared the city centre. The volume of traffic increased. A network of one-way streets and shopping malls made circulation difficult. The hotel was at the lower end of Wenceslas Square. The sixty-yard-wide boulevard was lined with restaurants, cafés, cinemas and office buildings. A doorman came forward, removing his cap as the taxi stopped in front of the art deco building. It was difficult for Raven to read the fare on the meter. The woman selected three bills from the handful he offered her and showed her gold teeth.

'*Dekuji!*'

The doorman carried their bags into an ornate lobby heavy with velvet drapes, deep couches and corniced walls. A pleasant-faced girl at the reception desk greeted them courteously.

'We have a reservation. The name is Raven,' he said. 'We'd like a room at the front if possible.'

She ran a coral-tipped fingernail down a page and nodded. 'How long will you stay with us, sir?'

'We're not quite certain as yet,' Raven said easily.

She reached for the passports. 'You may ask for these in the morning, sir. Please enjoy your stay with us.'

A teenage bellboy carried the two small bags to an old-fashioned hydraulic lift. He let them out on the third floor and opened their room with a flourish. Raven gave him a ten-crown note. The door closed gently behind him.

It was a large room with an eight-foot-wide bed. The pillows and duvet were enclosed in crisp lemon linen. There were two windows, each hung with velvet drapes, a writing-desk and a dressing-table with angled mirrors. A fringed lamp stood on the bedside table next to a pedestal telephone. A card printed in three languages informed guests how to obtain outside numbers. Raven followed his wife into the bathroom. The tub was encased in mahogany, the windows glazed with stained-glass panels. An armful of towels hung on a heated rail. They went back into the bedroom. Kirstie kicked off her shoes and spun. Her leap took her on to the bed. She bounced high a couple of times, her eyes shining. They lit on the flowers and fruit on the table.

'I love it,' she cried.

She pulled off her tank top and jeans, her breasts young and firm as she walked into the bathroom. She used the exaggerated gait of a model, hands bent out at the wrists as though testing the floor temperature. She gave a little backward kick, and closed the bathroom door. Raven pulled off his shoes and stretched out on the bed. Eleven years of living with her had been a constant battle of wills between them. Victory had never been certain. Her objection to what she called his manic obsessions continued but her claws no longer drew blood. They had achieved a sense of comradeship that was better than anything he had ever had before.

The difficulties he faced were enormous. He had no friends in the city and spoke not one word of the language. Even his credentials were suspect. Yet since the moment he had heard of Grattan's death, Raven had known he'd be coming here.

Kirstie emerged from the bathroom, her face washed, her hair neatly brushed. She stood in front of the dressing-table, using her lipstick. She spoke to his mirrored reflection. 'The light's looking good. I thought I'd go out with my camera.'

'Do you want to do something for me first?' he asked.

She adjusted the velvet beret. 'Sure. What is it?'

'Call the Canadian Embassy. Ask if you can talk to Lada Homolka.'

'We've been through all this before,' she objected. 'Why can't you do it yourself?'

'It's better if you do it,' he said. 'Tell her Dunbar was a friend of yours. Say that you saw him in London. Ask if you can meet after she's finished work.'

'But why *me*?' she insisted. 'I don't even know the woman. What am I going to say to her?'

'I know what I'm doing,' he retorted. 'I've got a feeling that she saw Grattan. In that case she might have something to hide. If a strange man calls she could be wary. A woman's different.'

She sat down at the bedside table. 'She's going to ask why I want to see her. I know I would in her place.'

'Say that it's something to do with Dunbar. A personal matter. Something you can't discuss on the phone. Don't even mention Grattan. Now just go ahead and do it.'

She lifted the handset off the hook. Raven leaned across in an attempt to listen to the conversation. All he could hear was what his wife said.

'Good morning. I'd like to talk to Miss Lada Homolka, please.' She rolled her eyes at her husband. 'I see . . . And you've no idea when she'll be back? . . . Thank you.'

She replaced the phone on its hook. 'She's been off sick.'

A bell rang in Raven's head. It seemed a bit too convenient, on leave *before* that and Grattan not killed on a Sunday – must have been a weekday. 'Look, why don't you do as you said, take a walk with your camera. I need to think.'

She looked at him suspiciously. 'Don't get yourself into any trouble. I'm supposed to be taking care of you, remember?'

He blew a kiss at her as the door closed.

He watched from the window until she came into view below, threading her way through the crowd of window-shoppers. And then she was gone.

It was twenty past two when he went downstairs. The lobby was crowded with Japanese. Raven spoke to the doorman. 'Will you get me a cab, please. I want to go the Canadian Embassy.'

The doorman beckoned. A taxi pulled forward.

77

Traffic moved at an orderly pace. There was no last minute burst at the lights, no blaring horns. Pedestrians waited until the signals released them. The cab crossed a bridge into narrow streets, past baroque churches and palaces. Cliffs of roofed terraces soared. Hradcany Castle and the cathedral dominated the skyline. The cab stopped outside a white stone building with a steeply pitched roof. Dolphins spewed water into a fountain. The cobbled courtyard was fronted by tall iron railings. The red, white, red of the Canadian flag stirred in the breeze from the river below. The taxi driver jerked his thumb.

'Canadian Embassy.' The gate in the embassy was locked. Raven pushed a bell marked VISITORS. A man in a dark suit emerged from a side door.

'We're closed,' he called.

Raven put his head against the railings. 'It's an emergency! I need to see Mister Wylie.'

The man sauntered across the courtyard, avoiding the spray from the fountain.

'Say again.'

'I have to see Mister Wylie,' said Raven. 'It's important.'

The guard made a further assessment of Raven. 'What's your name?'

'John Raven.'

The gate was unlocked. The two men walked into a vaulted hall with mosaic flooring. The security guard indicated a wooden bench. 'Take a seat.'

He was back again in a couple of minutes. 'Mister Wylie will see you now, sir.'

The door closed behind Raven. The man standing behind the desk was fifteen years younger than Raven, a sporty-looking character with short rusty-coloured hair and wide-framed spectacles. He was wearing tan trousers and a button-down shirt with a wide red stripe. His jacket hung on a coatstand near by. A fax machine hummed, ready to spring into action.

Raven sat down and chose his words carefully.

78

'Does the name Catriona Dunbar mean anything to you?'

'Sure,' said Wylie. 'We've corresponded. Her father's death was a great shock to us all. He was much respected in the department. Is that what your visit's about?'

'Not exactly,' said Raven. 'It's a little more complicated. You see, Catriona lived with someone called Henry Grattan. He was a friend of mine too.'

Wylie's face showed the first sign of caution. 'I'm not quite sure that I follow you,' he said.

'I'm trying to locate a Miss Lada Homolka,' said Raven. 'I understand that she works here. Can you give me her home address?'

Wylie bore his hostility openly now. 'I'm afraid I can't help you,' he said, rising. 'My advice is to go to the police if you want to know more about your friend Grattan. Your hotel will give you the right address.'

Wylie opened the door to the anteroom. The security guard came off the wall. 'The gentleman's leaving,' said Wylie. 'Make sure that he doesn't come back.' He slammed the door to his office.

The guard's face was expressionless. 'You heard what the man said.'

Raven made one last effort as they crossed the courtyard. 'I need Lada Homolka's address. I can make it worth your while.'

The guard opened the gate to the street. 'Take a hike!' he said, shortly.

Raven had to walk as far as Hradcany Square before he found a cab. Back at the hotel, he saw Kirstie sitting in a chair in the lobby. She smiled as he bent to embrace her.

'Don't look now,' she said, holding the smile. 'Don't look round but I think that girl at Reception is showing that man our passports.'

The man was in his late fifties, a burly figure with a massive head of grey hair and eyebrows. He was wearing a green velvet suit with a brown raglan coat slung round

79

his shoulders. He glanced briefly in the Ravens' direction and disappeared.

Raven walked across and leaned on the counter, smiling pleasantly. The two passports were no more than inches away.

'No problems, I hope?' he enquired.

'No,' she replied. 'Your passports were ready this morning. Is your room satisfactory?'

'The room's fine,' he said. 'The gentleman who just left, the one you were talking to. I've got the idea that I've seen him in London. Do you know if he's Czech?'

'I have no idea, sir,' she said. 'He certainly speaks Czech but I couldn't be sure. He was asking about a room.'

Raven walked back to his wife. 'She's lying,' he said, giving Kirstie back her passport. 'Let's get out of here.'

He took her arm and steered her towards the nearest lift. Upstairs in their room, he turned the key in the lock and left it there. 'I want to know why she lied,' Raven insisted. 'He certainly wasn't the house detective.'

Kirstie hunched her shoulders and kicked off her trainers. 'Curiosity, maybe. They're not used to foreigners yet. What happened at the embassy?'

He told her.

'But that's unbelievable,' she said heatedly. 'How *dare* they? Are you sure you didn't say something to upset them?'

'I'll tell you what I did,' he said, pointing a finger at her. 'I asked the right questions. I was watching Wylie's face. As soon as I mentioned Grattan's name, his manner changed.'

It was hot in the room. He turned down the thermostat.

'You know what the security guard said to me?' he demanded, stung by the memory. 'He told me to take a hike. I mean, I've read it a thousand times but nobody's actually said it to me.'

She patted the bed beside her. 'Come here and relax,' she said. 'You're letting this get to you.'

He closed the curtains and lay down with her.

'Do you want to go back to England?' she asked quietly, after a moment.

He rose on an elbow. 'No, I do not want to go back to England,' he said. 'We came here to help a girl who's in trouble.'

'I know that,' she soothed. 'But there's only so much you can do.'

'I was so *sure* about Lada Homolka. She's the one I have to get hold of. The embassy doesn't want any scandal. That's the truth of it, Kirstie.' He stared at the ceiling for a couple of minutes. 'I've got to get hold of that woman somehow.'

She felt for his hand. 'It's not your fault, lover.'

He refused to be mollified. 'Then whose fault *is* it for crissakes! I knew what the score would be before we came here.' He pounded his forehead. 'I can't go to the police for help. There must be some way of tracking her down. She's not in the phone book. I looked.'

'Sleep on it,' his wife said quietly. 'You've been on your feet since six o'clock this morning. We'll have a meal downstairs and go to bed early again.'

'That's exactly what we will do,' he agreed. It was good to let someone else take the decisions for once.

They had finished their meal. Kirstie was drinking coffee, Raven experimenting with a glass of slivovitz. The noise in the PA speaker was loud.

'Will Mister Raven please come to the nearest telephone.'

Raven put his napkin down and walked to the reception desk.

Catriona Dunbar's voice was distressed. 'I've been trying for hours to get hold of you. The flat was burgled this morning.'

'Calm down,' he urged. 'Where are you speaking from?'

'I'm upstairs,' she sniffed. 'It happened between ten and one. I didn't hear a thing. The burglar must have used a false key. The door wasn't damaged. But the place was an absolute shambles. Flour and salt and stuff all over the kitchen floor. They'd searched all the cupboards and drawers, gone through my correspondence. The weird thing is that nothing was taken. Not even the money my father gave me. I'm scared, John.'

A waiter was standing close. Raven turned his back on him. 'Have you been in touch with the police?'

'You told me not to,' she said.

'Good girl. OK. As soon as you get off the line, call Chelsea police station and ask for the CID. Explain what has happened. Don't mention me or the discs, Catriona. That's very important.'

'I won't,' she promised.

'Then do it,' he said. 'And as soon as the shops are open in the morning, call Banham's. Tell them you want all your locks changed. Are you still alone?'

'I am at the moment. A friend has promised to sleep here tonight. I'm waiting for her now. She says she'll stay for the next few days. Have you had any luck yet?'

He hadn't the heart to tell her the truth. 'There hasn't been much time,' he said. 'I should have some news tomorrow. Keep your chin up, hear now? I'll talk to you later.'

'I'll be waiting,' she said in a tiny voice. 'Goodbye, John.'

Raven went back to his table and told Kirstie what had happened.

He called for the bill. They were upstairs with the bedroom door locked before Kirstie spoke again. 'What do you suppose those thieves were looking for?'

'I know what they were looking for,' Raven replied. 'It's who was doing the looking that worries me.'

The curtains had been drawn, the top of the duvet turned back precisely. A flash of lightning lit the windows followed by a loud clap of thunder that rattled the frames. Raven extinguished the lights. They lay close in the darkness as the freak storm continued.

Chapter Seven

It was ten o'clock in the morning on the following day. They had eaten breakfast in bed. Kirstie turned away from the window. The hailstorm had washed the city clean. She dabbed scent on her wrists and slung her camera strap over her shoulder.

'I'm going to shoot a few rolls of film. How about you?'

He lifted his shoulders. 'I've got to try to find some way of getting hold of Lada Homolka.'

She waved goodbye from the doorway. 'I'll catch you later.'

He had shaved by the time the chambermaid came to clean the room. He left the hotel and walked three hundred yards to the Prague Information Centre. He took his turn in the line of tourists waiting for help. The girl who dealt with him spoke good English.

'I've got a problem,' he said. 'I've got this friend living in Prague but I can't find her home number in the book.'

She smiled. 'Foreigners do seem to have difficulties sometimes. What is the name of your friend?'

She searched through the telephone directory. 'I don't see it here. I'm sorry. The number could be in somebody else's name, of course. Do you have the address?'

He spread his hands, looking foolish. 'I left my address book in London.'

She leaned forward, showing him a place on the street map. 'I think the best idea is for you to go to the central police station. You'll find someone there who speaks English. They may be able to help you. It's not very far away.'

He nodded his thanks and turned left outside the building. The police were the last people he could go to for help. The pedestrian boulevard was crowded with people sitting outside the cafés in the pale sunshine. Raven turned back towards the hotel. Maybe Kirstie should go to the Canadian Embassy. Her passport must carry some sort of clout. His hope died instantly. As soon as Wylie heard her name she'd be finished.

A hand touched Raven's elbow from behind. He turned his head sharply. It was the man the Ravens had seen in the hotel lobby the previous night. The stranger fell into step.

'Please keep walking,' he said in perfect English. He pointed animatedly as a man would showing a visitor the sights of the city. His grasp remained firm on Raven's arm. Each step was taking Raven further away from the Gambrinus Hotel. He stopped in his tracks without warning. A couple of uniformed policemen were standing outside a bank twenty yards away.

'A waste of time,' said Raven's escort, maintaining his benevolent smile. 'We turn left at the next corner.'

The stranger seemed to favour his right side as he walked. Raven's first thought was that a gun was concealed in the other man's pocket. They passed a children's department store and a fast-food restaurant. The man quickened step to match Raven's gait. His grip slackened. 'In here,' he ordered.

Posters outside the theatre advertised INTERNATIONAL VARIETY SHOW!!!

The box office was closed. A piano tinkled inside the theatre. The stranger urged Raven into a dimly lit auditorium. A couple of spots were trained on the stage. A man was putting a line of girls through a dance routine. The piano player was down in the orchestra pit. No one paid attention as the two men walked down the side aisle. A baize-covered door led backstage. Sets built from

84

canvas and plywood were stacked in the wings. Costumes spilled out of baskets. A few steps led down to a row of dressing rooms. A woman was practising scales in one of them. The stranger indicated a door on the right and turned a key in the lock. Photographs of actors and actresses were stuck on the whitewashed walls. A large unframed mirror extended the length of the room. The make-up counter in front of it was streaked with grease-paint, the concrete floor littered with refuse. There was a strong stink of mice.

The man divested himself of his loose-fitting overcoat. He was wearing the same baggy green velvet suit as before, with a hand-knitted cardigan. He pushed a broken-backed cane chair in Raven's direction. 'My name is Teodor Brodsky,' he announced.

The cane chair creaked under Raven's weight. 'You were in the hotel last night,' he challenged. 'You were talking to the girl at Reception. My wife and I saw you.'

'That is perfectly true,' Brodsky said, smiling.

'Well, just what the hell do you think you're doing?' Raven asked hotly. 'Look, I've no idea who you are but you can't get away with this sort of behaviour.'

'No, no, no!' Brodsky said, holding a hand up. The backs of his fingers, his wrists, were covered with coarse black hair. 'Let me explain why I brought you here. I wanted us to be able to talk in privacy. The people outside won't bother us.'

Raven stared at him disbelievingly. 'I don't think you understand. I don't *want* to talk to you.' He took a shot at a laugh.

'It may not be what you want,' said Brodsky. 'It was my decision. We could have had this interview some-where else. A police station, for instance. I have that prerogative.'

'Really,' Raven observed sarcastically. He lit a Gitane with a display of bravado. 'Well, let me tell you some-thing, Mister Brodsky. I don't give a damn *who* you are. You can't just snatch people off the street like this. I'm carrying a valid passport. And as far as I know, I've done nothing illegal. You seem to think you have the right to question me. If that's really true, I want it done properly, in front of the British Consul.'

Brodsky chuckled. 'Of course. You of all people would know the correct procedure.'

'What's that supposed to mean?' Raven asked.

'Well,' said Brodsky, 'I know a great deal about you, Mister Raven. I know that you were a police inspector, for instance. You live on a houseboat in London and your wife is Canadian.'

'I've had enough of this charade,' Raven said. The computer disc was in his wallet next to his passport. 'I'd like to go back to my hotel.'

The Czech's face bore the look of someone presented with a show of childish defiance.

'Very well,' he said. 'In that case I will accompany you. Your bags will be packed and you and your wife will be taken to the airport. Tomorrow morning you will be placed on the first plane for London. Is that what you prefer, Mister Raven?'

Raven made no reply.

Brodsky's voice was persuasive. 'I think you should listen to what I have to say. I assure you that it is of the utmost importance. You have been making enquiries about Miss Lada Homolka. Miss Homolka was secretary to Mister Struan Dunbar, Trade Counselor at the Canadian Embassy here in Prague. Miss Homolka attempted to kill herself last night.'

Raven removed his cigarette from his lips. 'I'm sorry to hear it. Have you any idea why she should do something like that?'

'Despair,' said Brodsky. He chopped a twisted cheroot in half with a clasp-knife and lit one of the pieces. A cloud of acrid smoke wreathed his head. 'Her brother has been in prison for the last ten months. He worked in the state explosive factory. He was also a police informer,

86

something his sister had always refused to believe. She was shown proof of it yesterday.'

'I know nothing of that,' said Raven. 'I never even met the woman.'

'But your friend Henry Grattan did,' said Brodsky. 'Your purpose in coming here is no secret. You're a friend of Catriona Dunbar. You are here to try to arrange for Grattan's body to be returned to England. The Prague Criminal Police are not noted for their speed in such matters. I can help with this problem.'

'I see. And why would you do that?'

Brodsky fanned the air between them. 'Because your problem is linked to mine. I need your assistance. Do you know anything about my country's history, Mister Raven?'

'Very little,' Raven admitted.

Brodsky leaned forward. 'We suffered for forty-two years under the harshest form of Communist repression. Children were taught to inform on their parents, their teachers. They grew up like that, Mister Raven. The StB had files on everyone. Have you any idea what it means to live like that?' He dropped his cheroot on the floor and put his foot on it.

Raven shook his head. 'How could I?'

'How could you indeed,' said Brodsky. 'Only those who suffered can understand.'

An idea crystallised in Raven's consciousness. 'I think I know who you are,' he said quietly. 'You're part of Force Four or whatever you call it.' The thought somehow gave him confidence.

Brodsky's smile avoided the challenge. 'Just think of me as a friend. May I call you John?' The old-fashioned courtesy was endearing.

'Why not?' said Raven.

'Good,' Brodsky said benevolently. 'Do you believe in justice?'

'No,' Raven said promptly. 'I've seen it at work and it stinks to high heaven. That's why I left the police force.'

Brodsky tilted his head. His short legs and heavy shoulders made his movements cumbersome. 'How about a sense of fair play?'

'I never played cricket,' said Raven.

'Then what *do* you believe in?' asked Brodsky. 'How do you think that wrongs should be righted?'

Raven thought for a moment. 'Expediency, I suppose. The essential desirability for things to happen. It's the best I can do, I'm afraid.'

Brodsky continued to probe. 'Desirable for whom, exactly?'

It was a subject that Raven had often discussed. He had no problem with the answer. 'Basically for the causes and people I care about.'

'People like Catriona Dunbar and Henry Grattan?' asked Brodsky.

'I guess so,' said Raven.

Brodsky's dark eyes were steady. 'Might I be included?'

'It's possible,' Raven allowed. There was no doubt about the other man's sincerity. 'There must be a point to all this.'

Brodsky leaned forward again. 'There is. We need one another's help.'

Raven was beginning to enjoy the cut and thrust. 'Can you be more specific?'

Brodsky appeared to make a decision. 'There were six computer discs found on Dunbar's body. The Canadian Embassy sent them back to his daughter. Henry Grattan brought them to Prague. Like you, he stayed at the Gambrinus Hotel. I want to know where those discs are now.'

Raven was moved by a need to respond that was past all judgement. He reached inside his blazer and pulled out his wallet. The disc was in the back compartment. He gave it to Brodsky. 'This is one of them.'

Brodsky held it up to the light and inspected it narrowly. 'Where are the others?'

'They're safe,' said Raven.

'May I borrow this for a few hours?' asked Brodsky.

'Sure. I believe in playing my hunches. I'm counting on you to keep your word.'

Brodsky unsheathed his large nose from his fingers. 'Who do you think burgled Catriona's home?'

Raven laughed, his confidence won by the other man's frankness. It was like talking with an old and tried comrade. 'Whose phone did you bug – Catriona's or mine?'

'Yours,' said Brodsky. 'Every call that you've made since arriving in Prague has been monitored.'

'Did you know that the discs need decoding? You won't even get a picture up on the screen without.'

Brodsky's equanimity remained undented. 'There is no code that cannot be broken, my friend. The British proved that during the last war. All that is needed is the time, the expertise and the right kind of motivation. We have all these here in Prague.'

'OK,' said Raven. 'Tell me, what do you expect to find when you do break the code?'

'We're not sure. It could be any one of a number of things. But I can tell you where the discs came from originally. The StB, the old state security police who killed Henry Grattan.'

Raven sat as straight as he could in the rickety chair. 'Are you sure about this?'

'Certain,' said Brodsky. 'We cannot afford to make any more mistakes. You can help avenge your friend's murder, John.'

'Yes,' Raven said slowly. 'I'd like that.'

'The first thing is to give me your hand.' Raven complied. The grip was remarkably strong.

'We need your help, John. That's why I'm here,' said Brodsky. 'I am one of the people you spoke about. Force Four. Do you tell your wife everything?'

The idea brought a smile to Raven's face. 'Kirstie and I have a peculiar relationship. We don't lie to one another. But that doesn't mean that I tell her everything. I'd say that she knows that most of the time. She's been through a lot with me. The only thing that really worries her is my staying alive and well. After living with me for years it's understandable.'

Brodsky's face was regretful. 'I've never had the chance to be married. One day, perhaps.'

'Don't get me wrong,' Raven said quickly. 'Kirstie's a bright and intelligent lady. And we love one another dearly. She knows about the Dunbars and Grattan, the discs, for instance. I'm not sure that I'd want her to know any more.'

Brodsky pursed his mouth and nodded. 'Bear with me, please. When you've heard what I have to say you can make your decision. The general in charge of the StB at the time of the revolution was a dedicated Communist called Lorenc. He realised that change was inevitable. Political change. Economic change. Social change. The one thing he didn't foresee was the disbanding of the StB. When the writing appeared on the wall Lorenc acted swiftly. He ordered the destruction of all secret files held by the StB. It was one of the charges brought against him at his trial. His defence was that it had been done to prevent what he called "political misuse".'

'What happened to him?'

'They let him go,' said Brodsky. 'A pathetic figure without a friend in the world except for his wife. The point is that a number of these files were computerised before they were shredded. We know that there are more than two hundred. The ones you have are the first to surface.'

'And the others?'

A burst of shouting and laughter sounded outside in the corridor. Brodsky opened the door and bellowed in Czech. The noise ceased immediately. Brodsky stomped back to his chair.

'We just don't know where the others are. Or the codes to go with them. The man who approached Dunbar goes by the name of Milan Rotbart, a onetime pimp and an old StB informer. He's the man who shot Henry Grattan.'

'Then what's he doing walking the street?' Raven demanded.

Brodsky placed his foot on the half-burnt cheroot.

'For one thing, the only evidence against him is hearsay.'

'So what? You must know the people he mixes with, his associates.'

'You don't seem to understand,' Brodsky said patiently. 'We *need* to have Rotbart at large. We'll get nowhere without him. By now he will know that you're here, rest assured of it. And there's something else that is equally certain. It won't be long before he gets in touch with you. That's why we need your help.'

Raven's eyes widened. 'What would I have to do?'

'Whatever I tell you,' Brodsky replied. 'It's not an easy decision to make.'

'Can I think about it?' asked Raven.

'There's no time,' said Brodsky. 'I have to know now.'

Raven shrugged. 'I've already given you the disc. I don't like unfinished business.'

'Is that a yes or a no?' Brodsky insisted.

'It means yes,' said Raven. 'Where the hell did you learn your English?'

Brodsky stretched his short arms. Relief showed in his face. 'In England.' He pulled out a pocket watch on a nickel chain and consulted it. 'Will you and your wife have supper with me tonight? There will be one other guest, a lady. A very good friend of mine.'

'I think we'd like that,' said Raven. If Kirstie refused, so be it. 'What time would you want us?'

Brodsky came to his feet. 'At seven o'clock, if that's convenient. The Prospekt Hotel. It's a small place in the Old Town. Very few foreigners go there.'

'That'll be fine,' Raven answered.

Brodsky opened the door to the corridor. The rehearsal company had disappeared. The aisle lights shone on an empty auditorium.

'Do you think you can find your way back to your hotel?' Brodsky asked.

'First right, and then left,' said Raven. He had a strong sense of having done all this before but never with someone like Brodsky. 'Do you think I'll be followed?'

'I doubt it,' said Brodsky. 'But if you are, I'm sure you'll be able to deal with it.' He offered his firm handshake again. 'You've taught me a lot about human nature, my friend. I look forward to meeting your wife.'

The thought stayed with Raven all the way back to the hotel. The key to his room had already been taken. The door was locked when Raven tried it. He knocked.

Kirstie was standing inside in her stockinged feet. He fastened the door again and looked round the room. Her camera lay on the dressing-table. A couple of film packs bore stickers with the venue, shutter speed and the light exposure.

Kirstie looked at him curiously. 'What kept you so long?'

He drew her down on the bed beside him. 'I've got something to tell you,' he said.

'You haven't been back to the embassy again?' she said sharply.

'You're close but it isn't the answer.' He settled a pillow behind her back and lifted her legs across his knees. 'I left here this morning with one thing in mind. To get hold of Lada Homolka. The first place I tried was the tourist office. I told the girl there that I was on a business trip. I said I was trying to get in touch with an old friend who lived in Prague and I'd forgotten my address book. Was there any way she could help me. She couldn't find a listing for Lada. The best thing I could do, the girl said, was to go to the central police station. They might be able to advise me. Anyway, I started walking back to the hotel when somebody grabbed my arm from behind. You remember the man in the lobby last night – the one talking to the receptionist?'

92

Her leg muscles stiffened. 'The one who was looking at our passports?'

'That's him,' said Raven. 'He kept a tight hold on my arm and told me to keep walking.'

Alarm flared in Kirstie's face. 'Who *was* he for God's sake?'

'Well, he wasn't the house detective,' said Raven. 'It's difficult to say how I felt, Kirstie. A mixture of fear and surprise, I suppose. It was the way he acted that impressed me. It was as if he knew exactly what he was doing. All this was going on in broad daylight, remember, the street full of people shopping. Anyway, he took me into this clapped-out old vaudeville theatre and sat me down in a dressing room.'

He pointed across at his bag. The papers Sheffield had given him showed on top of his clothing.

'That pamphlet we read on the plane. The one about Force Four and all that? It's for real, Kirstie. This man is one of them.'

Her response was electric. She swung her legs from his lap and ripped the newspaper clippings and pamphlet in pieces. He heard her pull the chain in the bathroom. She came back and lit a cigarette.

'It isn't as easy as that,' he said. 'Let me tell you the rest of it.'

Raven had a good sense of narrative. It was easy enough to recapture the scene. His difficulty lay in explaining the effect Brodsky had had on him. Raven talked for the next fifteen minutes. Kirstie just listened. It was impossible to tell from her face what she was thinking.

She made sure that Raven had finished. 'Let me see if I've got this straight,' she said steadily. 'You're telling me that you gave the disc to this man, a complete stranger? The disc wasn't even yours, for chrissakes.'

'That's right,' he agreed. 'That's what I did.'

'Then you're out of your head,' she retorted. 'You're

93

putting us both in serious danger. Have you thought about that?'

'It occurred to me, yes. Brodsky's promised that we'll be protected. I believe him.'

She shook her head slowly. 'You're insane. OK, you're a grown man and that's what I married. I guess you have the right to do what you want to do. But you don't have the right to make decisions for me.'

'In that case you'd better start packing,' he said. 'Me, I'm staying. I've given my word to Brodsky.'

Her face froze. 'You and your goddam word!' she said bitterly. 'How many times have I listened to this?'

'It's one of the few things I've got that matters. You're the one who insisted on coming, remember?'

She dabbed at her eyes with her handkerchief. 'You bastard. All that crap about needing me.'

'I still do,' he said. 'Now more than ever.'

She took a deep breath. 'I wish I didn't believe what you've just told me. But I know you too well. It's true, isn't it?'

'Every single word,' he said. 'Look, we had a purpose in coming here, right? These people can help us achieve it. Why not give them a chance?'

She blew her nose hard, looked in her hand-mirror and raised her head.

'And what about you?' she persisted. 'God alone knows what they'll ask you to do.'

'I'll survive,' Raven said. 'I always have done. It'll be a lot easier if I know that you're with me.'

'You're a rat,' Kirstie said. A faint smile robbed the words of offence. 'You leave me with no alternative.'

He craned down, parting the soft blonde hair on the nape of her neck. He kissed her skin gently.

'I'll never ask you to do anything like this again,' he promised.

'You will,' she said. 'And I'll fall for it every time.' She put her camera back in its case. Her movements were brisk as she moved round the room, opening drawers and shutting them again. She stood in front of the long oval mirror, holding the black dress she had brought in front of her.

It was as if every word he had told her had been forgotten, but Raven knew better.

The Prospekt Hotel was an old-fashioned three-storey building on the corner of two streets in the Old Town. The ground floor was painted the colour of terracotta with arched windows. The upper floors were yellow. An elderly man with fierce side whiskers was writing at the reception desk. Brodsky came through the door from the restaurant. He was dressed in his green velvet suit. The fabric was worn at the knees and elbows.

He came towards Kirstie with both arms extended in welcome. It could have been an uncle greeting a favourite niece. He led her towards the restaurant entrance, her fingers resting lightly on Brodsky's arm. He held the felt curtain back, allowing the Ravens to precede him. His cardigan was buttoned lopsidedly under his jacket, his mane of grey hair tamed with pomade. The head waiter bowed to the Ravens and spoke in Czech to Brodsky. The party was led to an alcove table, reached by a couple of steps. The woman waiting for them was in her early sixties with dark-brown hair and pearl studs in her ears. She wore a fringed shawl around her shoulders, a red rose pinned to it. A similar flower lay on the plate on her left.

'This is Irena,' Brodsky said. 'And these are my friends from England!'

He took the rose from the plate and offered it to Kirstie with a courtly gesture. Kirstie sat on Brodsky's left, Raven on the right. Irena presided over the other end of the table.

Brodsky tucked a corner of his napkin into his shirt collar, wearing it like a bib. He leaned on his forearms, smiling at Kirstie.

'I hope you like pork, my dear.'

'Love it,' she said.

Brodsky's vast palm covered her hand. 'I have ordered a typical Czech meal,' he announced. 'Soup, roast pork and dumplings. And more dumplings to follow, the ones made with plums and served with sour cream. We will have to forget about diets, at least for tonight. Will everyone drink red wine?'

Raven was fascinated. His wife allowed few social familiarities. Brodsky showed no sign of being aware of it.

The restaurant was no more than half-full. The two tables near the alcove bore RESERVED signs.

Irena smiled lazily. 'Teodor has told me about you both,' she said, looking at Kirstie. Her English was good, her voice filled with the rich dark sound of a cello.

Brodsky waved assurance. 'You may talk freely in front of Irena. She is a very dear friend. She has been living in Austria for the last twelve years.'

'Whereabouts in Austria?' Kirstie asked politely.

It was Brodsky who answered. 'Irene was a political refugee. Her home here had been confiscated. Havel has just given it back to her.'

The two Czechs drank the soup in European fashion, using the pointed end of the spoon to direct the liquid into their mouths. Brodsky wiped his lips on his napkin and raised his glass. 'Your very good healths,' he said toasting each person in turn.

Raven continued to keep an eye on his wife. She was clearly fascinated by Brodsky. Raven recognised the pose. Head bent at a fetching angle, her eyes live with interest.

They talked their way through the meal without touching on politics. Raven took one sip of the thick Turkish coffee. It was enough. He refused Brodsky's offer of brandy and lit a Gitane.

Brodsky was smoking one of his Italian cheroots, solicitous that the smoke remained minimal.

'The idea is that Kirstie should stay with Irena for a few days,' he said casually.

96

Irena settled the shawl round her shoulders and rose. 'Perhaps we should leave them alone, my dear.'

Raven's wonder increased. Kirstie usually resisted any hint of patronage, especially from older women. Being addressed as 'my dear' provoked a sharp reaction normally. But here was his wife picking up her rose and following meekly.

Brodsky watched the two women as far as the exit. He relit his cheroot and spoke between puffs. 'Your wife is charming. What does she think about things?'

'I didn't go into details,' said Raven. 'There are a couple of things I'd like to tell you about Kirstie, Teodor. She was twenty-three when I met her. A girl from Toronto finding her feet in a difficult profession. She succeeded because she's good at her job. I'd just retired from the Met. God only knows what she saw in me. But whatever it was it's lasted. Since then she's come to terms with what she calls my derring-do. I know only too well how difficult it must have been for her. You and I talked about the things that make people act as they do – justice, expediency. What motivates me has got nothing to do with either of those. It's the thrill of the chase. It may sound absurd but it's true.'

Brodsky stubbed the cheroot into the ashtray. 'You're a man of integrity, John. And that matters far more than those other things. Now back to Kirstie. You'll find a message for you at the hotel. Kirstie has to return to London immediately. There is no direct flight to London until the morning. But there is a connection via Paris. Kirstie's name will appear on the passenger list. A car will collect her at nine fifteen. Instead of taking your wife to the airport she will be driven to Irena's apartment.'

'Sounds OK to me,' said Raven. 'At the moment she seems to be enjoying herself. Everything is strange and exciting. There's no real threat to her peace of mind. If it goes on like that she'll be convinced that this trip was her own idea. Believe me, I know the lady.'

Brodsky put his hand on his jacket pocket. 'My portable telephone. It's on permanent duty, under my pillow when I go to bed. You can reach me at any time. This is the number.'

Raven committed it to memory and put the piece of paper next to Brodsky's dead cigar. It burned in the flame from his lighter.

'I think I could do with that drink you offered me,' he said, smiling. 'Anything except slivovitz.'

The waiter brought a bottle of Hennessy and two balloon glasses. He poured with his left hand held behind his back. Brodsky watched him retreat and turned towards Raven again. 'What it is that's worrying you, John?'

Raven shrugged. 'The uncertainty. Not knowing who's going to come at me – or when.'

Brodsky's expression was thoughtful. 'I know no more than you do,' he said. 'But I am sure that the move will be made. It could be tomorrow, the next day, but soon. Rotbart will have made up his mind by now that you are the next likely customer. You will be offered some sort of arrangement. He may even talk about Grattan. I just do not know. But I am sure of this, John. He has no idea who I am or the fact that you have seen me. Our job is to keep him in ignorance.'

Raven shifted uncertainly. 'What about the hotel people?'

'There is no problem there,' Brodsky said firmly. 'No one will talk, rest assured of it.' The Czech had a way of dispersing difficulty that was hard to resist.

'But you'll be keeping an eye on things, right?' said Raven.

Brodsky smiled benevolently. 'An unblinking eye. As soon as anything happens, go to the nearest telephone and call me.'

The two men fell silent as the bill was presented. Brodsky produced money from an old-fashioned leather purse. He looked at his watch.

'It's getting late. I think you should go now.'

Irena and Kirstie were sitting by the fire in the annexe.

98

Brodsky rubbed his hands briskly. 'Our friends are leaving, Irena.'

The two women came to their feet. 'I will see you soon,' Irena told Kirstie. 'Goodbye, Mister Raven.'

Brodsky escorted the Ravens to the waiting taxi. He was gone when Raven glanced back. Kirstie snuggled close to her husband. 'I like them,' she said. 'Teodor's cute.'

'*Cute?*' Raven repeated. 'The drink's gone to your head.'

'You're just jealous,' she teased. 'Did you know he was a professor at the university here?'

'No,' Raven said.

'He reminds me of J. F. Kennedy,' she said. 'He's got the same sort of charisma.'

His nostrils narrowed. 'Apart from charisma, do you trust him?'

She sat very straight, looking at him in the light from the passing streetlamps. 'I trust him enough to let him take care of you. In my book that's trust.'

Her fingers stole into his hand and gripped tightly. Her loyalty made him feel guilty. He wondered if she'd be so enthusiastic about Brodsky if she knew what he had planned for Raven.

'That's all I needed to hear,' he said. 'Just as long as you're happy. It won't be for long and you'll have fun with Irena.'

'I'm still not clear what you two are going to be doing,' she said.

'Nor am I,' he answered. 'But you're better off out of it.'

The taxi deposited them outside the Gambrinus. The Japanese still milled in the lobby, about to set off on some cultural mission. Raven went to the desk for his room key. The girl found it and gave him a couple of envelopes. Both were addressed to Mrs J. Raven. She opened the telegram first and read it aloud to Raven.

ESSENTIAL YOU RETURN LONDON SOONEST STOP NO
DIRECT FLIGHTS THIS PM STOP TICKET VIA PARIS AWAITS
AT AIRPORT STOP TEMPLE.

The second message was from Czech Air Lines. They were sending a car to collect her at nine fifteen.

Raven looked at the clock. They had thirty-five minutes before the car arrived. Kirstie's face creased with dismay. He hurried her across to the lift. The cage began its ascent. Kirstie giggled mischievously.

'How was I?'

'Brilliant,' he said. 'You just earned an Oscar.'

They raced along the corridor. She started transferring things from the dressing-table into her flight bag. She stopped, scent-bottle in hand, looking down at the floor. There was a faint stain on the carpet. She put a finger to it and sniffed.

'Someone's been in the room, John. The bottle's been knocked over.'

'It's probably the chambermaid,' said Raven. 'She'd be too scared to tell you.'

She searched the drawer where her passport and traveller's cheques were, shaking her head all the time.

'Someone's been in the room,' she insisted.

He took a quick look through the drawers he was using. 'There's nothing missing as far as I can see.'

'My things have been moved,' she insisted. 'I can tell.'

He crammed the rest of her things into her bag. 'Come on, move it!'

They sat holding hands on a couch in the lobby. A Mercedes with a Czech Air Lines card in the window drew up under the portico outside.

Raven picked up Kirstie's bag. 'Let's go!'

She followed him out to the limousine. The driver was wearing uniform. Raven kissed his wife. 'Call me tomorrow.'

He walked back to the reception desk. 'My wife had to fly back to England,' he said.

The girl's face showed understanding. 'I'm sorry, sir. Will you be staying on?'

'For the next few days,' he said. 'I'll let you know in good time.'

He took a quick glance inside the bar. Three English businessmen were there, doing their best to avoid speaking to one another. Raven went back to the room. The stain on the carpet had evaporated. He had the chambermaid pegged as the culprit. He undressed and lay in bed in the darkness, thinking about Teodor Brodsky, the cause that he represented. It was a world outside Raven's experience, an *Alice in Wonderland* world where nothing was what it seemed to be. Yet strangely enough this was one of the reasons he was glad to be part of it.

It was twenty past eight in the morning and Raven had just finished his breakfast. The waiter from room service had opened the curtains on a grey cheerless day. Whatever talents Raven might have had as a policeman, patience had never been one of them. He went into the bathroom. Kirstie's forgotten nightgown lay on top of the laundry basket. It was weird to wake up and not find her lying beside him. He soaked in the tub for a while before shaving. The telephone trilled as he finished dressing. He picked the receiver up and sat on the side of the bed. A woman spoke in English.

'Is that Mister Raven?'

'That's me,' he said.

'I am sorry to disturb you at this early hour but it is an urgent matter. I am speaking on behalf of some friends, Mister Raven. They believe it will be to your mutual interest to meet one another.'

Raven's fingers tightened around the handset. The call had come sooner than he expected. 'Are you sure you've got the right person? I've only just arrived in Prague. I don't know anyone here.'

'Mister Struan Dunbar?' she said significantly.

'Struan Dunbar?' he repeated. 'Who's he?'

The woman made a sound of impatience. 'Please do not play games with me, sir. My friends are serious people. They have the material Mister Dunbar was looking for. They wish to know if you are interested in acquiring it.'

He let her wait for a while before he answered. 'Look, I don't discuss business over the telephone, still less with strangers. You'd better tell your friends that. I don't even know your name.'

'There is no necessity,' she said primly. 'I am simply conveying a message. Perhaps you need time to reflect. I will telephone again at eleven o'clock. Goodbye, Mister Raven and thank you.'

He looked at his watch. It was twenty-five minutes past eight. He opened the door to the corridor. A couple was checking out twenty feet away. The chambermaid's trolley stood outside the door. He heard the drone of a hoover. He hung the DO NOT DISTURB sign on the handle and relocked the door. He sat on the side of the bed and called Brodsky's number. The Czech answered against a background of noise.

'Brodsky.'

'It's me,' Raven said urgently. 'A woman just called. She didn't give her name but she spoke in English. She said she was talking for friends who had what Dunbar was looking for. They wanted to know if I was interested.'

'And what did you say?'

'I told her I didn't talk business over the phone, especially with strangers.'

'And then?'

'She's calling me back at eleven o'clock. Time for me to reflect as she put it.'

Brodsky's voice held a note of triumph. 'This is Rotbart, no doubt about it.'

'So what do I do?' Raven asked.

'You procrastinate,' Brodsky said. 'Tell her that any meeting must be in a public place. That is essential. I won't be very far away, John, rest assured of it. The other

102

thing that you must insist upon is that there must be no more than two people at the meeting. You and whoever they choose to send. Telephone me just as soon as you have heard from this woman and keep your messages short. This system tends to get overloaded.'

'OK,' said Raven. 'What news of Kirstie?'

'In excellent spirits by all accounts. I talked to Irena a few minutes ago. She is taking your wife to lunch with some friends of ours. Kirstie should find it interesting.'

'Well, give her my love,' said Raven. He cradled the phone and lit his first cigarette of the day. Talking with Brodsky was like taking a line of good coke. There was the same rush of adrenalin. He just hoped that the effects lasted longer.

The call came promptly at eleven o'clock. It was the same voice as before.

'Have you reached your decision, Mister Raven?'

'Yes, I have. There are two conditions. The meeting must be in a public place with only one person. If your friends will agree these terms, then fine.'

The woman spoke without hesitation. 'Leave your hotel now and turn right towards the Wenceslas statue. You must keep to the central walkway and proceed at a normal pace. My friends will take care of the rest.'

Raven tried Brodsky's number. It was engaged. He gave it a couple of minutes and tried again. The number was still engaged. Raven grabbed his trenchcoat and hurried down to the street. The central walkway was bordered with flowerbeds and shrubs. Crowds loitered on each side of the busy boulevard. He strolled north towards the statue, his senses alert for whatever might happen.

Most of the benches were full. A man sitting alone at one of them looked up as Raven approached.

'Mister Raven?' he said in English. There was a hint of a Cockney accent. 'I am the person you expected to meet. Please sit down.'

The man extended an arm along the top of the bench

as Raven obeyed. He was in his early fifties, wearing a black leather jacket and a woollen cap. His narrow-set eyes scanned the scene right and left. A couple of Carmelite nuns scuttled by, heads averted. The man spat on the ground.

'I think you know why I'm here,' he said.

Raven leaned back on the bench.

'I'm not sure. Why don't you tell me?'

The answer was unexpected. 'When did you last see Mister Dunbar?'

'The night before he left London,' Raven said steadily. 'He was my associate.'

The Czech's face hardened. 'That is what Grattan said. But he proved to be a cheat and a liar.'

'You don't have to tell me that,' said Raven.

The Czech was still watching the walkway. 'Do you know who I am, Mister Raven?'

'I think so,' said Raven.

'May I see your passport, please?' The man extended his hand.

Raven produced it. The Czech examined the photograph narrowly. He leafed through the pages, paying special attention to visas and entry stamps. He returned the document to Raven. 'My name is Milan Rotbart. Your passport doesn't mention your occupation.'

Raven lifted a shoulder. 'The British don't do that any more. Just the basic information.'

'But you travel a lot,' Rotbart insisted.

'I have interests in a number of countries,' said Raven. He placed a plate-glass window between him and Grattan's killer. Let Brodsky deal with it.

Rotbart's eyes were dead in his face, the eyes of a snake, unblinking and expressionless.

'What have you done with the computer discs, Mister Raven?'

This time Raven was prepared for the question. 'Five of them are in a bank in England. The other one I brought with me.'

104

Rotbart showed a row of nicotine-stained teeth. 'You haven't left it in your hotel room I hope.'

Alarm signals shrilled in Raven's brain. 'No,' he replied.

'I'm glad,' said Rotbart, discarding a shred of skin from his lower lip. 'I shall have to see it before we go any further.'

Raven assumed a display of indifference. 'Fine.' He looked at his watch. 'There is just one thing. I'm expecting a call from my wife. She had to go back to London unexpectedly. I don't want to miss her. Why don't we go to the hotel and continue our discussion there? We'll be able to talk in comfort.' He had to get hold of Brodsky quickly.

Rotbart shook his head. 'No,' he said firmly. 'That wouldn't be practical.' He pointed across at the Metro station. 'There are telephones in the booking-hall. You can call your hotel and leave a message for your wife. Say that you will be free in one hour from now.'

Raven hesitated. There was no way of refusing without arousing suspicion.

Rotbart was already standing. 'Come!' he said, showing his discoloured teeth again.

The two men descended the steps leading down to the Metro. The entrance hall was brightly lit, the floor covered with mosaics. Passengers were buying tickets from the vending machines. A display panel monitored the progress of trains. Rotbart indicated the row of payphones. Raven stepped into an empty one. There was no door on the booth. For a moment he thought that Rotbart was going to crowd in beside him. But the Czech was leaning against the wall, watching the steps to the street. Raven dropped a coin in the slot and dialled Brodsky's number. This time it answered.

'Trouble,' Raven said quickly.

'Stay calm,' Brodsky urged. 'I am in a car no more than fifty metres away. What happened?'

'Rotbart's asking to see the disc. He's standing just a

105

few feet away. He thinks that I'm calling the hotel. He already knows that I've got the disc with me in Prague.'

'How?' Brodsky asked quickly.

'I told him,' said Raven. 'He wanted to know where it was. What happens now?'

'You stay calm and do what I tell you to do.'

Brodsky spoke in Czech to somebody else. There was a noise of traffic in the background. Brodsky returned to Raven.

'Listen carefully, John. There's a café on the right as you leave the Metro. It's called Café Mozart. You can't mistake it – there's a stave of music painted across the awning. Your job's to get Rotbart in there. Make any excuse that you like as long as you do it.'

The booking-hall was crowded with passengers coming or going. Rotbart was still watching the steps.

'He's not going to let me out of his sight,' Raven said grimly.

'It doesn't matter. Just as long as you get him in there. You'll see a hatstand on the left as you go in. I want you to hang your coat on it and keep Rotbart occupied. Keep his attention away from your coat. When he asks for the disc it will be in your raincoat pocket.'

'Amen,' said Raven. 'And if it isn't?'

'You put your coat on again and play for time. Tell him you need to think things over before you part with the disc. I am in a black Mercedes parked behind the main tourist office. I can see the café from where I'm sitting. Help won't be far away if you run into difficulty. I'll stay here until I know what has happened.'

'I'll do my best,' said Raven. The phone went dead in his hand. He continued to talk for a few moments before replacing the receiver.

He limped through the crowds towards Rotbart. 'My leg's gone again,' he complained. 'I had an operation for varicose veins.'

Rotbart seemed unimpressed. 'Get the hotel to give you the name of a doctor.'

They climbed the steps to the central walkway. Raven could see the café, the front end of the Mercedes pulled as close as possible to the pedestrian zone. He came to a stop, wincing.

'It's no good,' he said. 'I'm going to have to sit down. Why can't we go in there?' he said, pointing across at the Café Mozart.

People were sitting at the tables out front.

'We'll take a look inside,' said Rotbart. He slowed his pace for Raven to follow.

The smoke-filled room was filled with noise coming from speakers on the walls. Men stood at the bar drinking beer. The hatstand was on the left in front of the lavatories. Rotbart chose a table near the entrance and called the waiter. There was a windbreaker and a white scarf on the hatstand. Raven hung his trenchcoat next to them and rejoined Rotbart. He put his tall frame between the coat and Rotbart.

'You think it's all right to talk here?' he asked, glancing round. Curtains blocked his view of the scene outside. The waiter brought coffee. Raven sniffed at it, wondering if the waiter belonged to Brodsky.

A lavatory door opened. A young man emerged and stood in front of the hatstand and started to comb his hair in the mirror. Finished, he slipped his arms into the windbreaker and wound the scarf round his neck. Rotbart's narrow-set eyes followed his exit.

Rotbart's voice was reproving. 'We have thieves here too, you know. Some of them make a speciality of stealing Western clothing. You should take more care of your belongings.'

Raven walked to the hatstand and picked up his trenchcoat. He could detect the shape of the disc through the fabric. He walked back to the table feeling more confident. He draped the trenchcoat across his lap and pulled out the computer disc. He placed it on the table between them. 'Don't worry, I had my eye on it.'

Rotbart held the disc in his hand briefly before returning it. 'I had to be sure,' he said. He was still wearing his woollen cap.

Raven dropped the disc in his blazer pocket. 'We all have to be sure,' he said.

Rotbart sipped at his coffee and put the cup down again. His tone was casual. 'Why did your wife go back to London?'

Raven pulled a Gitane from the pack, and lit it. He was completely in control of himself again and on the offensive.

'I'm going to say this before we go any further. I don't like your attitude.'

Rotbart's confidence slipped for the first time. Raven's outburst seemed to surprise him.

'I don't understand what you mean,' he said.

'I'll spell it out for you.' He pushed his coffee aside untasted. In the old days he would have been wired for this kind of dialogue. Brodsky must have his own reasons for not suggesting it. 'I don't know what kind of people you're used to dealing with. I'm here because you asked me to come. I've showed you my passport, you've seen the disc. Fine. But the question you've just asked is ridiculous. Let's get one thing straight here and now. I've put a lot of time and money into this enterprise. That doesn't mean that I'm not ready to cut my losses and drop the whole thing if I have to.'

'That would be foolish,' Rotbart said quickly. 'I'm here to do business. I am ready to listen to your proposals.'

Raven dribbled smoke from the side of his mouth. 'It doesn't work like that. You're the seller. It's up to you to say what your terms are.'

'A million dollars US,' said Rotbart. 'I give the codes for the discs Grattan stole. We can talk about further negotiations once we've got that out of the way.'

'A million,' Raven said pensively. 'That's not the figure that Dunbar told me.'

Rotbart's face resumed its customary belligerence. 'The

price has gone up. You can thank Mister Grattan for that. If it's too much for you, say so.'

Raven stared him out for a moment. 'It isn't the money. That can be found. But I shall have to consult my partner and I can tell you this much. He's like me. We'll have to be sure that we're buying the same information you offered to Dunbar.'

Rotbart picked more skin from his lip and got rid of it.

'I offered to put a picture on the screen. Dunbar never had a chance to see it.'

'I know that all too well,' said Raven. 'But you're not dealing with him any more. You're dealing with me.' It was like playing a game of chess. Each feint was followed by a countermove.

Rotbart adjusted his cap. 'How long will it take you to contact your partner?'

'I'll know that when I've talked to my wife,' said Raven.

'Is that why she went to London?' Rotbart said slyly.

'That's none of your business,' said Raven. 'Keep your mind on me. I should be able to give you an answer by nine o'clock tonight.'

'Take all the time you want,' said Rotbart. 'Just a plain yes or no is all that's required. But let me make one thing clear. There can be no bargaining about the terms. And rest assured that we will keep our side of the bargain. We are not like Grattan. We are men of our word.'

'It pays,' said Raven. 'It's the only way to stay healthy in my line of business.'

Rotbart pulled the woollen cap over his ears and paid the bill. 'You might as well finish your coffee. I'll see myself out.'

He was lost in the crowd within seconds. Raven waited a few minutes and walked to the black Mercedes. There was nobody in it. Brodsky was standing across the street. Raven joined him.

Brodsky touched Raven's arm briefly. 'Well done, John.'

Raven nodded. 'That's someone I could easily learn to hate.'

'We'll talk in a minute,' said Brodsky. He was wearing his tweed coat like a cloak round his burly shoulders. He lengthened his steps to match Raven's long stride. They turned left at the next corner and stopped outside the shabby façade of the vaudeville theatre. The entrance and box office were closed. Brodsky used a key on a side door. There was enough light to make out the rows of empty seats and the vacant stage. They walked down the aisle to the dressing rooms. Brodsky opened a door and found the switch. It was the same room they had been in on the previous day.

Raven lowered himself into the broken-backed chair. The remembered stench of mouseshit and greasepaint assaulted his nostrils. The cement floor was still unswept.

Brodsky removed his tweed coat from his shoulders and sat on the top of a clothes basket. 'We won't be disturbed here. Rehearsals don't start until one o'clock. Now tell me exactly what happened.' He put an elbow on his knee, his chin in his palm.

Raven told him. 'And that's about all there was to it,' he concluded. 'He's the sort of creep that birds fly backwards to get away from.'

Brodsky showed no surprise, as though he had heard it before many times. 'What did he say about Grattan?'

'Not a lot,' said Raven. 'He didn't even mention the murder.'

'He's hooked,' said Brodsky. 'Well and truly hooked, my friend. But he's a slippery customer and he's a long way from being landed. When you see him tonight, say that you have to go back to London.'

'London?' said Raven.

'That's right. There's been a change of plan. Tell me something. How does a man like you know if he's being followed?'

110

Raven frowned. 'Instinct, I suppose. I've never even thought about it. You get a sort of sixth sense. Why? Do you think you've got somebody on your tail?'

'Good heavens, no! Who in the world would do something like that? I'm a middle-aged teacher on a sabbatical.' Brodsky seemed to be enjoying himself.

The penny dropped. Raven took the computer disc from his wallet.

'Is this what you're worried about? You can have it back any time you like.'

'I don't need it,' said Brodsky. 'The cryptographer already has a copy.'

Raven tucked the disc back in his pocket. 'I thought you were worried about me being tailed.'

Brodsky summoned his genial smile. 'A lot has happened in the last few hours. You're going home tomorrow.'

The news punctured Raven's new-found euphoria. He was strangely deflated.

'Are you being serious?' he challenged.

Brodsky pursed his lips and nodded. 'You're wanted in London, John. You can tell Rotbart your partner won't talk any more on the telephone. You've got to go there and see him. Rotbart will have no objections. As far as he's concerned you're the man with the money. These people have hundreds more discs at their disposal. What concerns them is your real identity.'

'Just what the hell are you talking about?' Raven demanded. 'He *knows* who I am. The man's seen my passport. "You travel a lot," he said. What do you mean, my real identity?'

Brodsky held up his hand. 'Will you shut up and listen, please. You could be anyone. Your passport could be a forgery. I know what I'm saying, John. Your experience has been with a totally different sort of scoundrel. Rotbart was trained by the StB. These people trust nobody. It becomes part of their nature. Don't think for a minute that Rotbart believes all you've told him. He dare not,

111

especially after Grattan. They're going to dig deep into your background, find out what an ex-detective inspector is really doing in Prague. That's why it's necessary for you to return to London.'

The chair creaked as Raven sat up straight. 'That's great,' he said bitterly. 'For the first time in a long while I was beginning to think that I was really needed. What you have said proves I'm wrong. I'm a fool.'

'That's the last thing you are,' said Brodsky. 'If you were twenty years younger you'd be the kind of son I'd have chosen.'

'Thank you,' Raven said sarcastically. 'I'm not so sure about you as a father though. You're too bloody secretive. You keep things from me, Teodor. Things that I want to know. Things that I *should* know.'

'That's true,' said Brodsky. 'Most of the time it's because I don't know the answers myself. I'm having to learn as I go along. We'll just have to continue to trust one another. There's a man in London, a colleague of mine. He'll be getting in touch with you. I want you to give him the same trust and loyalty as you have given to me.'

'If it's a cop, forget it,' Raven said quickly.

Brodsky shook his head. 'He isn't a cop. He's someone who thinks the same way as we do. I talk to him every day. He knows all about you.'

'Who doesn't,' Raven said bitterly. It was the same old routine. The same glance through half-open doors. The same demands on his loyalty. Worst of all it was his same gut reaction.

He lit a cigarette. 'What about Kirstie?'

Brodsky relaxed. 'I've already talked to her. I said that you were needed in London. She seemed quite happy about it. She'll be home before you are. Your wife is an intelligent lady. She doesn't ask foolish questions.'

Raven rolled his eyes at the ceiling. 'That proves nothing. She'll have plenty of questions waiting for me when she sees me. I take it we are coming back here?'

'Oh yes,' said Brodsky, 'you are coming back. A few days, a week perhaps. It all depends on developments. Does this mean that we're friends again?'

Raven laughed in spite of himself. 'You should have been a conman instead of a teacher. You've got the same line of plausible bullshit.'

'But I don't have a larcenous nature,' smiled Brodsky. 'Do you think you can handle Rotbart tonight?'

'I haven't done too badly so far,' said Raven.

Brodsky pulled the nickel watch from his cardigan and consulted it. 'Time to go,' he said briskly. He tapped the phone in his pocket. 'Call if you are desperate. If not, I won't see you until tomorrow. I will be at the airport. You are booked on the eleven-fifty from Prague to Heathrow. A car will collect you at ten o'clock. That will leave us time for any last-minute discussions.'

He opened the corridor door and shouted. His voice echoed in the empty auditorium.

He placed both hands on Raven's shoulders and drew him into a bear hug. His clothes smelled of the foul cheroots he smoked. He let Raven go.

'Sleep peacefully, John, and remember. When the prison gates close on Rotbart and company we won't argue about expediency or justice. Just as long as they never come out alive.'

'I'll buy that,' said Raven.

He made his way out to the street and suddenly remembered that he was no longer limping. The pain came and went, he would say to Rotbart. The weird thing was it was true. He ate in a tavern and went back to the hotel. He collected his key at the desk. The same girl was on duty.

'I'll be leaving first thing in the morning,' he told her. 'I'll pick my bill up later.'

Back in his room he called his own number in Chelsea. Kirstie's voice came on the answering machine. 'I love you,' he said when the tone sounded. 'I should be home about one. I'll get a cab from Heathrow.'

He lay on the bed and closed his eyes. It was a strange thing about the boat. It was his real home, the place that would always draw him back.

He was watching television when the phone rang. 'Have you talked?' Rotbart asked.

'The answer is yes,' said Raven.

'I'm in the same place,' said Rotbart. 'Sitting outside. I'll wait.'

The scene had changed at the lower end of Wenceslas Square. The office buildings had closed. Nightlife had taken over.

CASINO HENRY BLACKJACK WE PLAY IN AUSTRIAN SCHIL-
LINGS DISCO CLUB GIRLS TARTAN BAR STRIP SHOW

The hookers were out in force, parading in front of the restuarants and cafés, posing in doorways. A midget was performing handstands for the line of cinema patrons. The interior of the Café Mozart was noisy. A football match was being shown on television. There were three people sitting outside under the awning, a bottle-blonde in tight jeans talking to a man twice her age and Rotbart at a table twenty feet away. There was a glass of beer in front of him. He looked up as Raven sat down.

'I'm flying to London tomorrow,' said Raven.

Rotbart's face showed nothing. 'So?'

'My friend needs to talk to me,' said Raven. 'There are things to discuss.'

Rotbart explored a back tooth with the tip of his tongue. 'What about?'

'The money,' said Raven. 'How you want it paid. Where. These things have to be arranged. You don't just walk into a bank and ask for a million dollars.'

'Do you know what a cashier's cheque is?' Rotbart asked.

'I know,' said Raven.

Rotbart continued. 'A cashier's cheque for a million

114

dollars drawn on a reputable bank. You'll deliver it here
to me personally.'

'That can be done,' said Raven. 'Does it matter if the
bank is English?'

Rotbart's smile was malicious. 'As long as it's genuine.'

The blonde and her friend left the neighbouring table,
their business arrangements concluded.

'You've got a strange sense of humour,' said Raven.
'I'd expect you to recognise a forgery. You'll take your
precautions and I'll take mine. I shall want to see something on the screen before the cheque's handed over. You
understand that, I hope.'

Rotbart nodded. 'I'll have everything ready. All I shall
need is twenty-four hours' notice as soon as you know
when you're coming back. Will you be staying at the same
hotel?'

'I'm not sure,' said Raven. 'How shall I get in touch
with you?'

Rotbart slid a piece of paper across the table. 'Call this
number and leave a message. And don't forget. I need
to know the day before. It's important.'

Raven put the phone number in his pocket.

'Don't feel that you're under pressure,' Rotbart said
encouragingly. 'I think we understand one another now.
Take as much time as you have to. The important thing
is the money.'

'It always is,' agreed Raven. He stood.

Rotbart's eyes had their laser-beam stare. 'You're not
limping any more. Did you see a doctor?'

'I rested,' said Raven. 'It's cheaper. You'll be hearing
from me.'

'I'll be waiting,' said Rotbart.

Raven merged with the crowd, making his way back to
the Gambrinus Hotel. He paid his bill at the desk with a
credit card. The girl gave him the carbon copy and smiled.

'I hope you enjoyed your stay with us. Please come
back again.'

'I shall,' he replied. 'Good night and thank you.' He

115

took the lift to his room and packed his bag, remembering Kirstie's nightgown. He was asleep within minutes.

It was the following morning. Raven carried his bag into the Departure Hall at Ruzyne Airport. The Mercedes that had brought him from the hotel was the same one that had collected Kirstie. A few passengers were standing in front of the one check-in counter open for international flights. Raven waited his turn. The Czech Air Lines hostess took his ticket and glanced at the screen in front of her. She tore a page from the ticket and gave him a boarding card.

'Just the one piece of hand-luggage, sir?'

'Just the one,' he replied. There was no sign of Brodsky. 'Are there any messages for me?'

She looked at the screen again. 'No messages, sir.' She pointed across the hall. 'If you'll go through to the Departure Lounge your flight will be called in half an hour.'

Raven had his passport stamped and passed through the security checks. He bought a carton of duty-free cigarettes and a couple of English newspapers. He sat down in front of the plate-glass windows. The Soviet-built Tupolev jet was outside on the tarmac, luggage bays open, the steps in place ready for embarkation.

Brodsky leaned over the back of the bench where Raven was sitting.

'I'm sorry I missed you outside. I was talking to someone.'

He sat down next to Raven. 'Did Kirstie call you?'

'If she did I was sleeping,' said Raven. 'Did she get off all right?'

'Yes, she did. She telephoned Irena about midnight. She had just arrived home.'

Raven pointed down at the other man's feet. 'Do you know that you're wearing odd socks?'

'It happens,' Brodsky said indifferently. 'I should buy

socks of one colour. It would avoid complications. How did things go with our friend last night?'

'The way that you said they would. I told him that I had to go back to London. He didn't turn a hair when I said that I might be gone for some days. All he was interested in was the money. He wants a cashier's cheque for a million dollars.'

Brodsky pulled a handkerchief from his pocket and blew his nose loudly. He wiped his eyes. 'Then we'll have to make sure that he doesn't spend his ill-gotten gains, won't we? Don't worry about that for the moment. Was there anything else of importance?'

Raven showed him the telephone number. 'He gave me this. He wants a day's notice once I know when I'm coming back.'

Brodsky looked at the piece of paper. 'I already know this number. It's a bar in the Old Town. They take messages for him. I spoke with my colleague in London. He'll be getting in touch with you some time tomorrow.' He rubbed his strong hands together, making a sound like sandpaper grinding.

'I'm not too happy about this colleague of yours,' Raven said doubtfully. 'Why can't you be more explicit?'

Brodsky put his hands on his knees and rocked for a while. 'He does the same sort of thing that I do, I suppose. But he has a great deal more experience. He's a professional. You'll find that you have a great deal in common. The same thoughts about a number of things.'

Raven was unimpressed. 'You know what he sounds like to me?' he said. 'He sounds like a spook, MI5 or something. One of the faces without a name.'

Brodsky's dark eyes twinkled. 'I'm sure that he'll give you a name. Why don't you be more tolerant?'

'Don't worry,' said Raven. 'I won't disgrace you.'

Brodsky's face sobered. 'He's a good man, John. You'll find out for yourself.'

A woman's voice came through the PA system. She spoke first in Czech then in English. 'Will passengers

117

for Czechoslovak Air Lines flight OK 754 to London Heathrow please go immediately to Gate Seven.'

Brodsky heaved himself up on his short sturdy legs. 'Keep the faith, John,' he said. 'We'll be in touch.'

Raven picked up his bag and the carton of cigarettes. 'Goodbye, you devious old bugger,' he said smiling. 'And watch your back.'

Chapter Eight

It was well after one o'clock when Raven paid off the cab that had driven him from Heathrow. He leaned on the parapet. The *Albatross* rode low in the water. Ducks foraged near the mud flats. Smoke from his neighbours' chimneys rose in the spring sunshine. The trees on the opposite side of the river were greener than he remembered.

He opened the door at the foot of the steps. Kirstie was lying on a couch in her jeans and one of his old fishing sweaters. She was reading a book. He tapped on the window. She was up on her feet when he came through the sitting-room door.

'Hi!' he said, pulling her close and kissing her. He held her at arm's length, smiling. Her hair was tied with a ribbon and she wore no make-up.

'You look about sixteen,' he said.

'I've been enjoying myself,' she said. 'Irena's a wonderful companion.'

He had his back to her, filling the dented silver cigarette box with the duty-frees. 'You know why we came back, of course?' He could see her in the mirror. Her face was untroubled.

'Irena told me,' she said. 'You've got to see some people for Brodsky. I find it all very exciting.'

He took his bag through to their bedroom. It seemed minute after the hotel apartment. A bowl of freesias scented the air. A clean pair of pyjamas lay on top of his pillow. He emptied his bag into the laundry basket, dirty shirts, socks and the nightgown that Kirstie had left behind. He put the computer disc, his passport, and some Czech crowns in the box where he kept foreign currency. He changed into jeans and a swanky new sweater. It was a relief to come home to a reception like this. There had been no reproaches or accusations. A couple of days with Irena Markova seemed to have blunted his wife's critical faculties. Long may it last.

She was still reading when he returned to the sitting room. 'What's the book?' he asked idly.

'*Theatre in Czechoslovakia.*' She put it down on the floor at her side. 'Are you hungry?'

'No. I had something to eat on the plane.' There was some post on top of his desk, letters that had been delivered during their absence. There was nothing of interest. He turned.

'Any messages on the Ansaphone?'

She sat up straight. 'I forgot to look.'

He switched on the machine. There were three messages on the tape. A reminder about paying his mooring fees, his own call from Prague and one from Catriona Dunbar.

'John, I tried to reach you this morning but the girl at the hotel said that you'd already left for London. I'm at home. Please call me.'

He turned the set off.

'I wish I'd heard you last night,' Kirstie said dreamily. 'It was sweet and kind and thoughtful.'

'Aren't you ladling it on a bit?' he said.

She shook her head. 'No. I mean it.'

He looked at her speculatively. 'You know what this is about, don't you? She's going to want to know what's happening with Grattan's body. What the hell do I say to her, Kirstie?'

His wife moved a shoulder. 'You tell her the truth. You can't do more than you're doing.'

He dialled. 'Catriona? Look, I just got your message. How can I help you?'

'Can you come round and see me, please?'

'Half an hour,' he said.

'She's a lucky woman to have someone like you to rely on,' said Kirstie.

'I don't know,' he said uncertainly.

She planted herself squarely in front of him, blocking his way to the deck.

'Listen to me. I won't ever refer to it again. I went to Prague with you because you told me you needed me. I didn't know then any more than you did what was going to happen. Force Four and all the rest of it. But I'm involved now and I'm glad of it. OK?'

'OK,' he replied and waited. There'd be more. Her eyes told him so.

'But I'm not a fool,' she went on steadily. 'Nor have I lived with you for eleven years for nothing. I realise there are things you're not telling me. Things I'm better off not knowing, maybe. I accept that. Catriona Dunbar's lost the man she loved. I'm not going to be put in that position.'

'You won't be,' he promised. 'If you'll only be patient with me. Look, if there are things that worry you, say so. You may not get the answers you want but I won't deceive you. That's a promise.'

'Fair enough,' she said. 'From now on we've got a new deal going. I don't ask questions and you don't lie to me.'

'A deal,' he agreed and donned his trenchcoat.

She adjusted the collar for him. 'Tell Catriona that any time she wants to come over here, she's welcome. Do you mind if I take the car?'

He shook his head. 'I'll see you later.'

He hailed a cab at the bottom of Oakley Street. The boutique was closed, Catriona standing in front of the maisonette doorway. She was wearing a black trouser-suit and looked less tense than when last he saw her. She hurried him up the stairs to the sitting room. A hoover hummed overhead.

'The girl who is staying with me,' said Catriona. 'She

121

won't come down here.' She closed the sitting-room door. 'Shall I make some coffee?'

'Not for me, thanks.' He faced her across the low table. 'What's the problem?'

'I'm not sure,' she replied. 'It's just that I had a visitor this morning. The doorbell rang just after eight o'clock. I thought it was the postman with a parcel or something so I went downstairs. There was this man standing outside. I'm not too good about guessing men's ages. I guess he was forty or maybe a little less. Well dressed and all that, the right sort of accent. He said that his name was Noel Baptiste, a friend of Papa's. He said that he wanted to talk to me.'

A flash of foreboding invaded Raven's thinking. 'And you let him in, I suppose. You've just been burgled but you still let him in.'

'Why not?' she demanded. 'He'd given me his card and my friend was having her breakfast next door in the kitchen. Don't be so snippy.'

'OK,' said Raven. 'What did he want?'

'We had a cup of coffee together. I left the kitchen door open and we talked. He knew that Papa was dead and told me how sorry he was. The last thing he wanted was to distress me, he said, but he did have this problem. He explained that he'd been doing some business with Papa and that he'd been left in some difficulty. He asked what had happened to my father's effects, said there might be something there that would help him. It was his manner that convinced me he was genuine. He was kind and considerate, not pushy.' She paused.

'So what happened?' asked Raven.

She shrugged. 'Nothing. I told him that whatever papers had been sent to me by the embassy were in the hands of my lawyer. He didn't seem at all surprised. All he said was that if I did think of anything that might help him, to give him a ring. That's when I started to be suspicious. I'd already told him I knew nothing about Papa's business affairs, that we'd been out of touch for some time. Anyway he just picked up his hat and said thanks for the coffee and left. I thought I did the right thing.'

'You did,' said Raven. 'Have you still got the card?'

She opened the long drawer in the bookcase and pulled out a visiting card and an envelope.

He studied the card.

Noel Baptiste
Baptiste Enterprises Ltd
465 Dover Street
London W.1.
Telephone 071 491 0902

'And this?' he said, tapping the envelope.

'They're the things that were found on Papa's body.'

He slipped the visiting card inside the envelope. 'Leave this to me,' he said. 'If he calls again just hang up on him.' His eyes strayed to the photograph on the mantelpiece. 'Did he mention Henry at all?'

For a moment she seemed on the verge of tears but controlled herself.

'No,' she said sadly. 'I've been trying to come to terms with all that. It isn't easy but I am trying. I just can't bear the thought of him lying forgotten in some mortuary. I want his body back here,' she insisted.

'I'm working on it,' he assured her. 'I've met some good people in Prague, people with influence. They're helping me. I'm going back to Prague in a few days' time. Meanwhile there's always the phone. Kirstie told me to say you should call her whenever you feel like it.'

They came to their feet together. 'You're good friends,' she said. 'I hope that some day I'll be able to repay you. I'm glad that Kirstie came back with you. It's no good to be away from the person you love.'

He pulled her close on impulse and kissed her cheek. 'You'll be just fine,' he promised. 'You're good-looking and gutsy. There aren't too many like you around. You'll get by, believe me you will.'

His next stop was at Companies House. He paid the search fee and took the requisite file from the records. Baptiste Enterprises Limited had been formed in 1986. The name of the secretary was given as Jocelyn Gaunt with an address in Wimbledon. Noel Baptiste was the only director. The articles of association were brief. 'All forms of general trading.' Raven returned the record and used one of the payphones outside in the lobby. Kirstie was out. His call activated the Ansaphone. The only message was from Jerry Soo.

'Phone me. It may be important.'

Raven searched for another coin. Jerry Soo and he went back twenty-two years. They had started their police careers together at Hendon, a couple of misfits, each with his own particular problem. The Hong Kong cop was the first Chinese to join the Met. Raven's cross was his background and accent. The two men bonded immediately. They went fishing together. Raven was best man when Soo married a girl from Taiwan, a cellist with a London chamber orchestra.

Raven used the direct line that came through on Soo's desk.

'It's me, Jerry. How are you?'

'We're fine. How about you two?'

'Fit and well,' said Raven. He hesitated. A number of lines at New Scotland Yard were bugged in the name of internal security. 'Can we talk or have we got Uncle George taking notes?'

'We can talk,' said the detective superintendent. 'I keep up with what's happening. Listen! I had occasion to go up to the sixth floor yesterday. That asshole Drummond was in the lift, the one who you used to say looked like a whorehouse bouncer. He always makes a big thing of asking about you whenever I see him. He doesn't come on too strong but you can always detect the poison dart in his fist. He made a point of telling me that your file had been pulled "again" as he put it.'

The service records of Metropolitan police officers were kept long after they had left the force. Raven's file was removed at least twice a year.

'Who was it this time?' he asked.

Soo's voice was amused. 'Special Branch. You must be going up in the world.'

'I'm a legend,' said Raven. 'Perhaps they're going to give me a testimonial.'

'I wouldn't hold your breath,' said his friend. 'I just thought you might like to know. If I hear anything more, we'll talk. OK?'

'Cool,' said Raven, 'and thanks, Jerry.'

He replaced the handset, his face thoughtful. It could be coincidence. If not, Jerry would tell him.

He spent the rest of the afternoon in the Reference Room at Chelsea public library. There was no listing for Noel Baptiste in any of the business registers. A disembodied voice at the Law Society informed him that the solicitor who acted as company secretary had died the previous year. The voice had no knowledge of his replacement. Raven found a cubicle free and switched on the reading-lamp. The envelope that Catriona had given him contained a statement from a bank in Toronto showing a credit balance of twenty-eight thousand dollars and forty-nine cents. There was a snapshot of Catriona in a Hermes wallet, Dunbar's driving licence and car insurance. A letter from a woman in Paris, a book of Prague Metro tickets. There were no addresses or telephone numbers. Nothing to indicate that Dunbar was anything more than what he purported to be, an undistinguished employee of the Department of Foreign Affairs.

Raven scooped the papers back in the envelope. The streetlamps came on as he neared the cul-de-sac opposite his boat. Kirstie wasn't back yet. The car was missing. A bell tinkled as Raven opened the door to the shop. His neighbour was sitting on a Javanese prayer stool, his legs wrapped in a dungaree jacket. He had shaved off his beard and was growing a pony-tail. That and the granny-glasses gave him a passing resemblance to the late John Lennon. The room stank of incense and the joint Lauterbach was smoking. The Californian offered it dreamily.

Raven refused. 'Did Kirstie mention when she'd be back?'

'No,' said Lauterbach. 'But you do have a visitor. He was in here asking which was your boat.'

'And I suppose you told him,' said Raven. The junk in the place never failed to depress him. Brass artefacts and dusty bales of Indian cotton, cheap rings and sandals. Paper parasols, an endless array of stuff doomed to be trashed wherever it ended up.

'I told him zip,' said Lauterbach. 'Right now he's parked out in front of the pub. A dark-blue Fiesta.'

Raven nodded at the joint in the other man's fingers. 'Is that all you do all day?'

'When I've got it,' his friend said placidly. 'Otherwise I just sit. How was it in Prague?'

'You wouldn't like it,' said Raven. 'Too strenuous. Bye-bye.'

The Waterman's Arms faced the river. It was a pleasant pub with Dickensian associations. There was a carpark out front and a few trees, with a dark-blue Fiesta parked under them. Raven went into the bar. The landlord was leaning his stomach against the counter.

'Yes, squire,' he said. 'What can I get you?'

'Nothing,' said Raven. They were old sparring partners. The friction between them had gone on for years. The landlord was an ex-policeman who never lost an occasion to show his disapproval of Raven. Raven nodded back at the car parked outside. 'Have you any idea who owns the Fiesta?'

'Nope,' said the landlord. He drew himself a half-pint of beer and held the glass to the light.

'Come off it!' said Raven. 'You're not the sort of person to let people use your parking space without

126

making sure that they buy a drink. You'd be out there clamping their wheels.'

The landlord put his glass down very carefully. 'You asked me a question, mate. You don't like the answer, take your questions somewhere else.'

Raven walked to the end of the carpark. There were four lines of traffic along the Embankment, most of it going westward. He peered through the Fiesta windows. An A-Z road atlas lay open on the passenger seat, a half-empty roll of peppermints next to it. There was a car-phone attached to the dashboard. Raven tried all four doors, aware that the landlord was standing at the window, watching him. The doors were locked. Raven waited until signals halted the traffic. Then he threaded his way through the lines of immobile vehicles. A man was leaning over the parapet taking flashlit photographs of the *Albatross*. Raven tapped the back of his shoulder.

The man turned round sharply. He was twenty years younger than Raven with a sturdy body under his stone-coloured raincoat. He looked Raven up and down. 'You've got to be John Raven, right?' He produced a press card bearing his photograph and the name Acme News Service, Chancery Lane, W.C.2.

'Paul Messenger,' he said. 'I'm doing a piece on Henry Grattan.' He pushed his free hand out.

Raven ignored it. 'Never heard of him,' he said.

The reporter smiled ingratiatingly. 'Knightsbridge Crown Court, nineteen seventy-nine? Look, I've read the report. Detective Inspector John Raven. You were the arresting officer. All I need is a quote. You know, something about Grattan's murder, the way you felt when you heard about it, that kind of thing.'

Raven moved swiftly, grabbing the camera from Messenger's hand and removing the roll of film. He tossed the film into the river below and returned the camera.

'Piss off!' he ordered.

Messenger's expression was shocked. 'That was totally

out of order,' he said. 'You don't need to act like an animal.'

'Take a walk,' said Raven. 'If not, I'll make you wish that you'd never heard of me.'

Messenger put his camera back in its case. 'You know where to come if you change your mind.'

Raven watched until the Fiesta headlamps came on. Then he ran down the steps to the gangway and opened the sitting-room door. Raven lifted the phone.

'Acme News Service,' a woman's voice said.

'Have you got a reporter by the name of Messenger?' asked Raven.

'We don't have any staff reporters,' she answered. 'We're an agency. We just buy and sell material.'

'Well, there's somebody who's using your name,' he said. 'and he's making a nuisance of himself. My name's John Raven. You'll find the address in the book. Tell your boss if it doesn't stop, I'll be making a complaint to the Press Council.' He slammed the receiver down.

It was twenty to six. The traffic was building up along the Embankment. It would continue like that until early morning brought total silence. Down on the boats it was quiet in the fast-fading light. He switched on the pedestal lamp and closed the curtains. Kirstie had left a note. *Gone to see Maggie. Back about six.*

He smiled to himself, remembering her face that morning. There'd been no melodrama. But a few seconds had given them a new respect for one another. He went into the kitchen. It was a large room with a stainless-steel sink under the blue-and-white checked curtains. The refrigerator and freezer were next to the sink. The raw pine table was big enough for six people to sit at. A dresser and four large cupboards matched the table. Raven put his weight against the end of the freezer. It rolled back on wheels, exposing a hatch in the floor.

He lifted the hatch. A cowled lamp lit a short companionway and the hold below. Timbered framework supported the cedarwood superstructure. Raven used the

128

hold as a cellar. He went down the companionway backwards, his hands gripping the rails tightly. Bilge washed through the scuppers below. He took a couple of bottles of claret from the racks and carried them up to the kitchen. He pushed the freezer back in place and raised the lid. It was empty except for some plastic containers labelled in Mrs Burrows's tortured scrawl. She made a point of cooking whenever the Ravens were absent, a reminder that she had once taken care of him in his bachelor days. The results was always inedible.

He was in the sitting room watching the news when Kirstie stormed in. She pulled off her velvet beret and shook her hair free. Her voice was exasperated.

'That *bitch*! Everything you do for her is wrong. I'm not sure I can take it much longer.'

She hung her Burberry in the closet and put a shopping bag down on the kitchen table next to the wine.

She sat on the couch next to him, her voice casual. 'I see you've been down in the hold,' she said casually.

'Just a couple of bottles of red,' he said. The unlicensed thirty-eight he had kept there had long been discarded but she still remembered it. 'What are we going to eat for supper? There's nothing in the freezer, I looked.'

'I bought some calves' liver,' she said. 'But if you want onions you'll have to peel them yourself. The bread trick never works for me. My eyes still smart and I dribble.'

He squeezed her knee. 'I'll fix us a couple of Bloody Marys.'

He opened the drinks cupboard. A light came on inside. He tipped tomato juice into the tumblers, dropped in a few ice cubes and added two fingers of Polish vodka. He carried the drinks to the couch. He raised his glass. 'To what we agreed this morning. No secrets, no recriminations.'

She took a long pull at her drink. 'OK, you go first.'

'Catriona,' he said. 'A man rang her doorbell at eight o'clock this morning, someone called Noel Baptiste. He said he was a friend of her father and wanted to talk to her. She's got this girl staying so she let him in and they talked. He explained that he'd been in the middle of doing some business with Dunbar but he hadn't kept any records. He assumed Dunbar's things had been returned to her and wanted to know if she'd found any papers that might help him.'

'But why let him in?' Kirstie objected. 'A stranger. You wouldn't catch me doing it. Did he ask about the computer discs?'

'Not a word,' said Raven. 'Grattan's photograph is up on the mantelpiece. He didn't even look at it. Catriona told him that all her father's papers were in the hands of the lawyers.'

'Well, at least that showed sense,' said his wife. 'So what happened?'

'He said that when she did have a chance to go through the papers to keep him in mind. If she did find anything she thought might help, to get in touch with him. Then he gave her his card and left.'

Kirstie swirled the ice in her glass with a finger. 'Couldn't this be the buyer? The man Dunbar was going to sell the discs to?'

Raven sank his drink. 'I don't think so. I mean, why just talk about papers? Why not even mention the discs? Catriona says he seemed perfectly genuine at first. We don't know what Dunbar had going. It could be anything.'

'I don't like the sound of it,' said Kirstie. 'Have you told Brodsky?'

He shook his head. 'We've only been back a few hours. We can't call him every time something goes bang in the night. I checked Baptiste's company. It's kosher.'

He took their empty glasses to the cupboard and spoke with his back to her. 'The other thing was that I talked to Jerry. The Special Branch pulled my personnel file yesterday.'

Her fingers were still at her throat when he turned. 'Oh *nooo!*' she wailed. 'We're not going to start all that again?'

130

'It could be no more than coincidence,' he said. 'Jerry's going to let me know if he hears any more.'

She looked at him narrowly. 'There's something else, I can tell.'

'Nothing of any importance,' he said. He reached in the box for a cigarette. 'Did you tell Hank Lauterbach that we'd been to Prague?'

She nodded. 'Sure. It was hardly a secret. Mrs Burrows knew for one thing. I said we'd been over there arranging about a friend's funeral. What's wrong with that?'

'Nothing,' he said. He rounded his mouth and attempted a smoke-ring. He felt like a fish out of water and failed. 'It's just that some reporter was asking him which boat was ours. Hank says he didn't tell him but he's been out of his skull all day. I found the guy leaning over the parapet taking pictures. He knew that I'd busted Grattan and wanted a quote.'

'So you hit him,' Kirstie said quietly.

'Perish the thought,' he said. 'But I did take the film from his camera. I don't think we'll be hearing from him again, somehow.' He shrugged. 'And that's about it.'

She finished her drink and stood up. 'I'm going to take a bath. You can lay the table for supper.'

'I won't just lay the table,' he said. 'I'll cook the liver.' He looked at his watch. 'Supper will be served at a quarter to eight precisely.'

He took pains with the preparation, marinating the liver in salt, pepper and lemon juice. He found dried onion flakes in the spice cupboard and opened a can of young peas. He spread one of his aunt's fine cloths on the table, lit candles and turned off the electric light. The liver would only take five minutes to cook. He returned to the sitting room and caught the last of the news on Channel Four. He was glad to be home. He was glad to be with Kirstie. And most of all he was glad of their new understanding. The news ended. He put a Mozart tape on the player. He donned Mrs Burrows's apron to protect his new sweater and rattled a spoon in an empty jug.

131

Kirstie came through as he started to serve the food. She was in her towelling-robe, pink from the bath and wearing his emerald matrix heart between her breasts. They sat down across the table from one another.

'Good food and wine, music and a beautiful woman,' he said. 'What more can a man ask for?'

She had washed her hair and her eyes were bright. 'A little English mustard, maybe?'

They ate leisurely, without much conversation. They finished one bottle of wine. They were drinking coffee when the phone rang on the dresser. Kirstie reached behind her and took the call. 'For you,' she said. 'A man.'

Raven took the receiver. 'John Raven.'

'Good evening. I am Teodor Brodsky's friend. Do you know Old Queen Street in Westminster, Mister Raven?'

'Yes, I do. It's not too far from the underground station.'

'That's the one. Number 14B. Can you be there at four o'clock tomorrow afternoon?'

'Yes.'

'Then I'll see you there then. Goodbye, Mister Raven.'

Kirstie cradled the phone. 'Who was it?'

'Brodsky's friend. I'm seeing him at four o'clock tomorrow. Did the voice mean anything to you?'

She shook her head. 'No. Why?'

'I don't know. I'm sure I've heard it somewhere before.'

She turned down her mouth. 'I certainly haven't. It's the phone. Voices often sound different. Let's go into the sitting room.'

They carried their coffee through. She sat beside him, her fingers kneading the back of his neck.

'I was thinking,' he said. 'That money that Dunbar left in the bank in Zurich. It belongs to Catriona now.'

'It won't be easy to get it,' said Kirstie. 'You know what Swiss banks are like.'

The tide was on the turn and the boat wallowed gently.

'All it needs is the right lawyer. Patrick would probably know of one.'

'Ask him,' said Kirstie.

'I thought you could do it.'

'Why me?' Her fingers continued massaging his neck muscles.

'You could say you had this friend whose father had died in Switzerland. Tell Patrick what's happened but don't mention Catriona's name. Or mine, come to that. Tell him you don't want me to know about it.'

She made a face. 'OK. I'll call him now.'

She spoke on the phone for a couple of minutes and put it down. 'He'll see me at ten in his office.'

He made sure that the security bolts on the door to the deck and the windows were fastened. He yawned.

'You want me to help with the washing-up?'

She caught his yawn and covered her mouth. 'No, I'll get it. I think I'll stay here and watch the box afterwards.'

'I'm going to read,' he said. 'Don't worry about the television. It won't disturb me.'

The bedside lamp was out long before Kirstie crept in beside him. He fell asleep with the voice on the phone still eluding his memory.

Chapter Nine

Raven raised himself on an elbow. It was ten past eight by the travel clock on the bedside table. Kirstie had pulled back the curtains and was moving around in the kitchen. He padded after her in his pyjamas. The table was laid for one. Toast in a napkin, a pot of Earl Grey and two boiled eggs in a Humpty Dumpty holder. Kirstie had collected the post and the newspapers from the box at the front of the steps. She was standing under the window applying the last of her make-up. It was the same as she normally used in daytime. A little eye shadow, blush, and coral lip gloss that toned with her fingernails.

He sat down heavily, rested his chin on his palms and looked at her. She was wearing a black tailored suit, white silk shirt, flat patent pumps and her black velvet beret.

She blotted her mouth with a tissue. 'Brodsky called earlier.'

The strong tea cleared the fog from his brain. There was an hour's difference in time between Prague and London.

'Why didn't you wake me?' he said.

'Because Brodsky said not to. He said for you to call him back any time during the next two hours.'

He stared at the egg he had just decapitated. The white always disgusted him.

'All that fuss,' said his wife. 'You eat the white when it's scrambled.'

'That's different,' he said. 'What time are you going to be through with Patrick?'

'It shouldn't take long. He's got to be in court at a quarter to eleven.' She put her cup in the sink and aimed a jet of scalding water at it. 'Don't forget Mrs B's here this morning.'

'I won't,' he assured her. 'I'll be off the boat before she gets here. How about having lunch together?'

She dropped the car keys in her handbag. 'Where?'

'The Black Bull in the Fulham Road? We can eat upstairs in the gallery.'

'I'll see you there at one,' she said.

The door banged at the end of the gangway. The spring was supposed to have been fixed a week ago. He left the eggs uneaten on the table and went into the sitting room. He looked at the calendar on his desk. The cleaning lady worked mornings one week, afternoons the other. She appeared at any time after ten, bent on discussing some current disaster. If none sprang to mind she invented. She tried Raven sorely but she was part of his life.

He took the phone in his lap and dialled Brodsky's personal number.

'Good morning,' said Brodsky. 'Are you alone or not?'

'I am but it wouldn't matter,' said Raven. 'Kirstie and I have got a new deal going. No more secrets between us. It's better that way.' It was good to hear the Czech's voice again.

'I agree,' said Brodsky. 'I'll bear it in mind. I gather my friend has made contact.'

'I'm seeing him this afternoon,' Raven was hesitant. 'I don't know how important this is but Catriona Dunbar had a visitor.'

'I know about that,' said Brodsky. 'It's under control. I'm going to be in Vienna for a few days so we won't be in direct contact. That doesn't matter. Talk with my friend. It's the same as talking to me, John. You must give him your total confidence.'

'Whatever you say,' said Raven.

'As long as that's understood,' said Brodsky. 'He'll keep you informed. In any case, you'll be back here very shortly. Goodbye John, and take good care of yourselves.'

Raven redialled. Catriona Dunbar came on the line.

'I looked through that stuff you gave me,' he said. I'm trying to get hold of a lawyer to take care of your father's Zurich account. Have you got any papers to prove your relationship with him?'

'I've got everything,' she said quickly. 'His passport, my birth certificate, things like that.'

'I want you to get them Xeroxed,' he said. 'Do it right away. Put the copies in an envelope with my name and address on it and send them round to the boat. Any time after eleven o'clock will do. I'll be back then. OK? I'll talk to you some time later.'

He shaved in the shower and dressed in his blue double-breasted suit, a pale-grey shirt and black brogues. He climbed the steps and took a bus to Victoria Street. He turned left past St James's underground station then right to the corner of Old Queen Street. The gracious houses represented part of London history, they were protected by conservation orders. People no longer dwelt in them. The houses had long been used as prestige offices by firms of architects, civil engineers and charitable organisations. The neighbourhood was deserted after seven o'clock at night.

He strolled towards 14B. It was a three-storey building with railings in front. A lead flat blocked off the basement and area steps. The exterior was plain dark brick. The windowframes had been enlarged and painted white. Gauze curtains made it impossible to see through the glass. A flight of steps led to a solid oak door with a fanlight above it. A closed-circuit television camera the size of a shoebox was angled at the street from the wall under the fanlight. There was a brass plate and a bell on the left of the door.

Raven walked as far as St James's Park. Tourists and children were feeding the ducks on the lake. Gulls swooped in competition. He found a seat on a bench and mulled over the implications of what he had just seen. Retrospection had never been one of his strongest suits. Brodsky must know what he was doing. Otherwise they could be in serious trouble. New Scotland Yard was a quarter of a mile away. Jerry Soo was up there somewhere. It would have been good to talk to him. But there was no chance of that. Not right now anyway. A phrase from the past invaded his memory, the parting salute from a man about to be sent back yet again to prison. 'It ain't the cards you get that matters, it's the way that you play them.'

Raven took a bus back to South Kensington. He walked up Fulham Road. Kirstie was waiting in the gallery café above the Black Bull. She was at a table near the end wall. He sat down across from her.

'How did it go with Patrick?'

She had finished her cauliflower cheese and was drinking Coke. She dabbed her lips with her napkin.

'He didn't say much. He was in a hurry. There's nothing can be done from here, he said. We'll need a Swiss lawyer, someone who handles this sort of thing. He gave me the name of a man he knows.'

She gave him a card.

Klaus Breitweg   DL, Harvard
76 Spielstrasse
Zurich 1

Raven put the card in his pocket. 'Catriona's sending some papers round, birth certificates and the like. Did Patrick say anything about Grattan?'

'Not a word,' she said. 'I told you, he was in a hurry. What did Brodsky want?'

The waitress was hovering. 'I'll take the same as my wife,' he said.

He turned to Kirstie again. 'He already knew about Baptiste. He's going to be off the air for a few days. He made a point of saying that this friend would take care of everything for the moment.'

'You don't seem too happy about it.'

'It isn't the same,' he replied. 'We'll just have to wait and see what he's like.'

The waitress brought his meal. The cheese sauce was the way he liked it, strong and runny. He pushed his plate to one side and lit a cigarette. 'I had a stroll along Old Queen Street this morning. There's some kind of bullshit plate on the door. Something to do with planetary research and a closed-circuit television hanging outside on the wall.'

Her eyes brightened. 'Really? How exciting! I can't wait to hear what's inside.'

'We'll know soon enough. What are your plans?'

'I'm going to do something I've not done in years,' she answered. 'A matinée. There's a film on at the Cannon that I want to see.'

'I'll walk you down,' he said and called for the bill.

They walked arm in arm, not bothering to talk any more, content to be close.

Mrs Burrows was still on the boat, polishing silver in the kitchen. She was wearing rubber gloves that stretched as far as her elbows and the butcher's apron. She nodded across at the envelope on the dresser.

'That came by taxi about an hour ago. The man wouldn't say who sent it. And another thing, one of your aunt's silver teaspoons is missing.'

He closed the bedroom door firmly and ripped the envelope open. Inside was a copy of Struan Dunbar's passport, Catriona's birth certificate and a registrar's record of her parents' marriage. He put the Swiss lawyer's card in with them and locked the envelope away in the bureau drawer. He ordered a radio cab for three thirty and hid himself in the guestroom.

Raven glanced at his watch and placed his thumb on the doorbell. A full minute elapsed before the door was opened by a middle-aged man with a short-back-and-sides haircut. His neat grey suit fitted him like a uniform. He scrutinised Raven thoroughly.

'Sir?'

'My name's John Raven,' he said. 'I have an appointment for four o'clock.'

A wide cream-painted stairway rose from the panelled and thickly carpeted hallway. Photographs of aeronauts hung on the walls. There was a board at the foot of the stairs.

ADMINISTRATION
PLANETARIUM
LIBRARY

'Please come this way, sir.'

Raven followed his escort down a corridor to the rear of the house. A ten-speed mountain bicycle was propped against the wall near a door. A pair of steel cycle clips was attached to the handlebar.

Raven's escort tapped on the door and opened it. 'Your visitor, sir.'

The door closed gently behind Raven. Michael Sheffield rose to greet him. He looked a lot different from when Raven had seen him last. Gone was the business suit and bowler hat, the umbrella. Sheffield was wearing slacks and a cricketing sweater. There was a Jack Russell terrier on the floor near his feet.

'My God!' said Raven. 'Not you again!'

'I'm afraid so,' said Sheffield, grinning amiably. 'Take a pew. Do you have a problem with dogs, Mister Raven?'

'Not unless they have a problem with me,' said Raven.

The room was sparsely furnished. There were no book-shelves or pictures. There were two canvas-backed chairs of the sort used on film sets, a wide draftsman's table with a leather case on it. The windows were heavily veiled. A shaded DayGlo lamp provided the only light. Sheffield pushed an ashtray in Raven's direction.

'I can imagine how you're feeling, but it had to be done this way. I might as well tell you, when your name first came up I was against the choice for what I thought were obvious reasons. Events proved me wrong. Brodsky has nothing but praise for you.'

Raven's mind was still reeling. 'Did Patrick O'Callaghan know about this?'

'Not a peep,' said Sheffield. 'Like you, I imagine, there are large areas in my activities I keep to myself. We knew you were going to Prague. If you hadn't asked Patrick for help we'd have had to have found an alternative.'

'What about that pamphlet you gave me, Force Four and all of that?'

'That was Brodsky's idea. The printing chaps worked overtime. I have to ask this question. Are you ready to give me the same trust you've given Brodsky?'

Raven sought an honest answer. 'I respect Brodsky. If you're working with him that's enough for me.'

'Good one,' Sheffield said pleasantly. 'Well, now that we've got that out of the way, I'll fill you in on what's happening. Anything that I ask you to do while you're here will be done with Brodsky's approval. Most of the planning is his anyway. The first thing I have to say is keep away from Noel Baptiste. This is important. Let me deal with him. I understand that Catriona Dunbar is a friend of yours?'

'I'm taking care of her interests,' said Raven.

'Of course.' Sheffield's smile stretched the cleft in his upper lip. 'You know about Miroslav Salin, I take it?'

'The Czech delegate to the Interpol Conference. Ex-Communist, speaks German and English fluently, the first

140

they've sent since the end of the war. Brodsky told me something about him, yes.'

Sheffield inclined his head. 'That's the bugger. He arrived a couple of days ago. Well, the first thing he did was make a beeline for our delegate. He made no bones about what he wanted. He explained that Prague was full of people supposed to be businessmen. He said that the Brits were his main concern. On the one hand his country needed all the help they could get from the West but the possibility of something dodgy was always there. The Czechs had no files on these people, no way of separating the wheat from the chaff. He said he didn't want to make a nuisance of himself but was there any way that our friend could help him?'

Raven lit a cigarette. 'Sounds reasonable enough.'

'It is,' said Sheffield. 'The new boy, charming and eager to please. Anyway, our man was sympathetic. He said he'd have a word with his superiors and see if there was anything that could be done. Then Salin came up with a couple of names of people he said they were specially interested in. The first was Henry Grattan, you were the second.'

'Did he give any reason?'

'He said that Grattan had been killed in peculiar circumstances and that you were known to be a friend of his. Our chap did exactly what he had said he'd do. He took the whole thing upstairs. Have you ever seen your G2 file, Mister Raven?'

'I've never even *heard* of a G2 file,' Raven admitted.

'You've been away a long time,' said Sheffield. 'It was started five years ago to keep tabs on people who left the Met with question marks hanging over them.'

'I didn't have any question mark hanging over me,' Raven said heavily. 'I got out because I didn't want to serve under a bunch of senior officers who were on the take.'

Sheffield opened the leather bag. A sheaf of papers and photographs slid across the table. He selected a type-

written sheet and gave it to Raven. 'Take a look at this,'
he said. Raven picked it up.

G2 INTELLIGENCE UNIT
(This report has been extracted from Personnel file
BY/8465/8398/JR ACCESS RESTRICTED TO
AUTHORISED OFFICERS) *Subject* Raven, John

Raven joined the Metropolitan Police Force 3/2/
62 Resigned 21/3/74 Raven currently resides on a
houseboat in Chelsea, London S.W.3. Raven
inherited the estate of a maternal aunt August 1968
(probate value £364,836).

Raven is believed to have funds in Switzerland,
Luxembourg and the Cayman Islands. The Internal
Revenue reports no irregularities in Raven's tax
returns.

No records have been found to suggest any legit-
imate business activities.

Raven travels extensively and is believed to have
contacts with known arms dealers. Extensive enquiries have failed to produce viable evidence of Raven's
involvement in any illegal activities.

Harold Cleveland
Detective Superintendent

'What is this shit!' said Raven. 'I could sue the bastards
for this.'

'I wouldn't advise it,' said Sheffield. 'I'm responsible
for everything you see in front of you.'

Raven was still shaking his head. 'My aunt would spin
in her grave if she knew about it.'

He picked up the first of the photographs. The high-
definition print featured him leaving a KLM plane in
bright sunlight, dressed in a white suit, panama hat and
wearing dark glasses. A sticker on the base of the print
identified the venue as Damascus, 5 May 1987. The other
three photographs were similar in character. One showed
him standing outside the Victoria Street offices of the

Iranian Purchasing Commission. Yet another had him getting into a cab with a man dressed in Arab clothing. In the last he was seen boarding Adnan Khashoggi's yacht in Monte Carlo.

These were examples of high-tec forgery. Scale, focusing and background were perfectly matched. There was no possibility of detection.

Sheffield watched silently as Raven picked up the telex.

MESSAGE REFERENCE 2741 FROM DD AAR 86 ATTN J Raven
We have available two tons Semtex explosive with detonators and fuses. One hundred portable rocket launchers surface to air (SAM) missiles. The price for the above merchandise is US dollars five million ($5,000,000). This offer is not divisible.

Best regards Safur.

Next came what appeared to be a memorandum of a telephone call from the Syrian consul in Hamburg to an unidentified correspondent.

Advise Raven his offer accepted. Complete sale soonest and inform this office.

Raven pushed the documents back to Sheffield. 'What the hell are you trying to do to me?' he said bitterly.

Sheffield swept the documents back in the leather bag. 'Salin's been given copies of everything. Grattan's CRO file was straightforward, just the date of his arrest and conviction. But you know what they say, if you lie down with dogs you get fleas. Isn't that right, Tiger?' He leaned down and pulled the terrier's ear.

Raven rearranged his long legs. 'Am I getting this right – you're saying that Salin is part of Rotbart's bunch of villains?'

'I'm saying it's possible, probable even. The conference doesn't finish for two more days. What happens between

143

now and then will prove me either wrong or right. If Salin does as I think he will, you should be hearing from him.'

Raven found the idea disturbing. 'You know I've got my wife on the boat? I mean, OK, for once in her life she's got a fair idea of what's happening, but I'm not going to put her in danger.'

'No.' Sheffield's hand chopped a hole through the suggestion. 'There won't be anything like that, I assure you. If Salin does get in touch he'll be pleasant enough. As far as he's concerned you'll be a potential business partner. Added to which I'll always be there in an emergency.'

He scribbled a telephone number on the inside of Raven's cigarette pack. 'Call me any time of the day or night. I'll get the message.'

'Another one who sleeps with the phone under his pillow. It must restrict your social life.'

'I try not to let it worry me,' Sheffield said, smiling. 'We call it customer service.'

'Uhuh,' said Raven. There was something irritating about the way Sheffield fielded his objections. 'Have you thought about this, then? Rotbart's seen my passport. I'd need a visa to get into Syria. I've never had one.'

Sheffield's voice was indifferent. 'A man like you can be expected to have more than one passport.'

Raven put the pack of Gitanes in his jacket pocket. 'And the money? I'm supposed to be showing up in Prague with a cashier's cheque for a million dollars. Where's that going to come from?'

'I've got an idea that Mister Baptiste might produce the answer to that one. That's why I want you to stay away from him. If not, we'll have to resort to the slush fund. When the stakes are high enough, Her Majesty's Treasury can be generous, especially if they're sure of getting their money back.'

Raven shook his head. 'No more questions,' he said. Events had their own weird logic.

Sheffield slid a printed form across the table. 'That just

144

about wraps everything up, then. If you'll just put your moniker on that, I'll let you get back to your wife.'

Raven stared down at the form disbelievingly.

'Official Secrets Act. You've got to be joking! I signed one of these things when I joined the Met.'

'This is different.' Sheffield produced a fat-barrelled Shaeffer. 'You might want to write your memoirs.'

Raven grinned in spite of himself. The man had a sense of humour. He affixed his signature and looked up.

'Do you fish?' he asked.

'Fish?' Sheffield echoed. 'No, I don't. But I wouldn't mind trying. Why do you ask?'

Raven pushed the form back. 'I go with a friend every year to the Norwegian fjords. We try to catch salmon. It's wet and it can be cold but it is exciting. If you can ever find the time, you might like to join us.'

He had an odd urge to find out how Jerry Soo and Sheffield would react to one another. Jerry Soo with his innate dislike of disorder, Sheffield with his indifference to it.

'I'll bear it in mind,' said Sheffield. 'I really will. It just might work.'

He took Raven's hand in both his own. 'Don't forget, any hour of the day.'

He opened the door and called along the corridor. 'My guest is leaving now, George. Have the kindness to show him out.'

Raven paid off the cab in front of the steps leading down to the boat. The spring on the door at the end of the gangway had been fixed. Kirstie was on a chair in the sitting room, Raven's Zeiss binoculars in her lap. She made a habit of watching the birds at dusk, how they suddenly vanished to roost.

He wiggled his fingers at her and went straight through to the bathroom. He flushed Sheffield's telephone number down the bowl. It was already stored in his memory bank. He changed into his cords and sweater

145

Chapter Ten

Miroslav Salin was in his bedroom in the Holbein Hotel in Pimlico. He was over six feet tall with a full head of greying black hair, a short nose and a misleading smile. An admirer of English tailoring, he was wearing a Jaeger check suit he had bought on arrival. He was forty-two years old.

Born in Brno, the only child of a factory manager and a German-speaking teacher from Sudetenland, Salin had passed through the state school system with honour. He spent two years at Bratislava University studying economics. At the age of twenty-one he joined the StB and was posted to the Ministry of the Interior.

In 1989 he was arrested for crimes against humanity and defended himself in court. He pleaded that he had always been a conscientious servant of the State, a man who only obeyed orders. It was a time when a new concept of justice allowed for leniency. Salin was released. Aware of his need to be rehabilitated, he worked for six months as a street-cleaner. He joined the Prague Criminal Police and was given the job of organising Czechoslovakia's new Interpol office. Since then his promotion had been rapid.

He picked up the phone and asked for an outside number. A girl's voice answered.

'Baptiste Enterprises Limited. May I help you?'

Salin's English was colloquial and fluent. 'I'd like to talk to Mister Noel Baptiste, please.'

'I'm afraid he's on another line at the moment, sir. Shall I get him to call you back or will you hold?'

'I'll hold,' he said.

A man's voice came on the line. 'Noel Baptiste speaking.'

'My name's Miroslav Salin,' he said. 'Does the name Struan Dunbar ring a bell?'

There was a pause. 'Who did you say you were?' asked Baptiste.

'I'm Czech,' said Salin. 'I think we should talk. I don't have a lot of time. Could I see you at five o'clock? I'd rather not come to your office.'

Baptiste's voice sounded puzzled. 'Can you give me some idea what it is you want to talk about?'

'Not on the telephone,' said Salin.

'Very well,' Baptiste said. 'We can meet in the Royal Automobile Club in Pall Mall. If you'll be there at five o'clock, I'll be waiting.'

Salin relinquished the telephone, smiling.

It was the penultimate day of the Interpol Conference. The main body of work had been dealt with. A motion was put to discuss the position of new member states. Salin spoke from the podium. He had come to London, he said, with great hope for the future. He was leaving full of assurance. He pledged his country's full co-operation and left the platform to loud applause. He received it modestly, exchanging addresses with new acquaintances. He presented the British delegate with some Bohemian crystal supplied by the embassy and made his adieux.

The entrance to the club was imposing. The lobby had the hush of a cathedral. A uniformed porter stood at a desk on the left. Members were taking afternoon tea.

A man came from behind a pillar. 'Mister Salin?' he enquired. 'I'm Noel Baptiste.'

Baptiste looked younger than Salin had expected, with reddish hair. His grey flannel suit carried an elegance that Salin appreciated.

'We'll go down to the reading room,' said Baptiste. 'We'll be quiet down there.' It was a room of noble proportions with leather chairs, newspapers and an open fireplace. It was empty.

Salin lowered himself into a seat with his back to the window. Baptiste sat down opposite.

Salin displayed his official delegate card with his photograph and name on it.

'I'm here in good faith,' he announced, 'so I'll be frank with you. I work for the Prague Criminal Police.'

Baptiste smiled nervously. 'What do the Prague Criminal Police want with me?'

Salin gave him smile for smile. 'I'll try to explain. I'm not here in an official capacity. I'm here as a friend. You were involved with Struan Dunbar, the Trade Counselor at the Canadian Embassy. You visited his daughter after his death. Is that right?'

'Hold on,' Baptiste said quickly. 'I'm not sure I should be answering these questions. I mean, who the hell are you, anyway?'

'Look,' said Salin, 'if my presence here is bothering you, I can always leave.'

Baptiste's face reddened. 'I don't know how you came by this information but I can assure you that nothing I've done is illegal. The last time Dunbar was in London he came to me with a proposition. I agreed to finance it. There was a record kept of our conversation. I was told that Dunbar's personal effects had been returned to his daughter. I wanted to know if she'd found anything among Dunbar's papers that might help me. She said the papers were in the hands of her lawyer. I run a straightforward business, with a good reputation. Struan Dunbar was on the point of retiring. There was a possibility of him joining us as a part-time consultant. It's as simple as that.'

'But you did invest money in Dunbar's proposition.'

'A great deal of money,' said Baptiste. 'It may sound

absurd on the face of things, but it happens to be the truth.'

Salin leaned forward. 'Has it ever occurred to you that you may be the victim of a confidence trick?'

Baptiste stiffened visibly. 'Are you saying that Dunbar was a crook?'

'No,' said Salin. 'But some of his daughter's friends may be. A man called John Raven, for instance. A known associate of some very unprincipled people. Not the sort of man someone like you would want to do business with.'

'I never even heard of the man!' Baptiste said vigorously.

'But you might,' Salin said gently. 'I'm a Czech. We have a duty to people like you, sir. If there are any more questions you'd like to ask, I'll be at the Holbein Hotel until the day after tomorrow.'

Baptiste was twisting the signet ring on his little finger. 'I'm not used to this sort of thing,' he said. 'But thanks for the tip.'

Salin looked at his watch. The interview had taken less than twenty minutes. 'I have to go now,' he said. 'I've enjoyed meeting you. If you ever come to Prague look me up. I'll be glad to be of any assistance I can.'

The two men climbed to the hallway and shook hands perfunctorily.

Salin took a taxi to an office supply store in Oxford Street. He left two thousand pounds poorer.

It was early afternoon. Raven sprawled on the sofa staring across at the windows. Rain had been falling since early morning, gurgling in the drainpipes and gutters. Even the gulls were silent. Raven was bored and dejected. He had not moved off the boat in two days, reluctant to let anyone else near the phone. Sheffield had called just once to say that Baptiste had met Salin in a club in Pall Mall. There was no news from Brodsky. It was hard for Raven to contain his resentment. He had the feeling that he was

151

being excluded. Prague was fast being erased from his memory.

Kirstie made light of his despondency. He had to be patient, she told him. She busied herself cooking his favourite meals, did her best to keep out of his way, cosseted him. Without her the tension would have been unbearable. He checked the clock. Kirstie had been making the rounds, seeing magazine editors and her agent. With any sort of luck, she'd be back soon.

The telephone shrilled at his elbow. 'John Raven,' he said.

The upper-class drawl was slightly nasal. 'This is Noel Baptiste, Mister Raven. I think we should talk about Struan Dunbar, don't you?'

Raven straightened his back. 'When did you have in mind?'

'Would it be all right if I came round now – or do you have someone with you?'

'I'm alone,' said Raven. 'Are you driving?'

'Yes, I am. Is there somewhere to park?'

'There's a pub across the street from our boat. You can leave your car there.'

'I'll be with you in just a few minutes,' Baptiste promised.

Raven used Sheffield's emergency number. 'I'll have to make this short. Baptiste just called. He wants to talk about Struan Dunbar. He'll be here any moment.'

Sheffield was jubilant. 'We've cracked it! Now listen. We'll only get one bite at the cherry, John. So watch it. Call me back the moment he's left. I'll be waiting.'

Raven ran to the kitchen windows. There was a partial view of the traffic coming west along the Embankment. A blue Saab appeared, indicating a turn to the right. The car pulled in close to the trees. The driver emerged holding a newspaper over his head. The buzzer sounded a couple of minutes later. Raven released the door at the end of the gangway. Baptiste came into the sitting room, his shoes and trouser-bottoms flecked with mud. He

152

dropped the soggy newspaper in the wastepaper basket and sank down on the coach.

Raven gave him a box of Kleenex.

'Shall I get you a coffee or something?'

Baptiste shook his head. He glanced round the room and lighted on the picture of Kirstie on top of the desk. He grinned. 'You look nervous. Don't be alarmed, there's no reason.'

'I'm not nervous,' said Raven. 'Just curious.'

Baptiste mopped some more at his trousers. He looked up, his tone condescending.

'I can explain. You're a wily old bird, but I know where you're coming from. When you get down to basics, you and I have a lot in common.'

'Such as what?' Raven asked. Years of experience had sharpened his nose for larceny. This man's heart was stuffed full of it.

'Struan Dunbar?' said Baptiste. 'You know you behaved very badly. You surprised me, a man with your track record.'

'I tend to have that effect on the uninstructed,' said Raven. This oaf needed a jolt to his ego. 'You said you wanted to talk about Struan Dunbar. Why don't you do it?'

Baptiste's aristocratic nose thinned. 'I will. Dunbar did a deal with a friend of mine. You stole their property.'

'*Stole?*' said Raven. 'You don't seem to have much of a grasp on reality. Whatever deal you might have had with Dunbar is history. Dunbar's dead. I inherited. It's as simple as that.'

Rain lashed at the window, the sound loud in the sudden silence.

'What's the matter?' asked Raven. 'What happened to your concentration?'

Baptiste pulled himself together. 'We're both men of the world,' he said placatingly. 'OK, you've got the discs. But they're useless without the codes. And you don't have the money to buy them.'

153

Raven stretched his mouth in a smile. It was good to be rolling again. 'You're making another of your doubtful assumptions, my friend. You don't *know* what I've got. The people in Prague, for instance. I'm the only one left that they'll talk to. They trust me.'

Baptiste glanced at the clock. It was a quarter to three. 'There is a way out,' he said. 'Think of it as the start of a brand new chapter. I'd like you to meet a friend of mine, hear what he has to say. If you don't like the sound of it, there'll be no harm done.'

'Who is this friend?' Raven asked.

Baptiste rearranged the folds in his trousers. 'He's a busy man. Why don't you put your coat on and I'll take you to see him?'

'OK,' Raven said easily. 'There are a couple of calls that I have to make. You go on out to the car.'

Baptiste already had the door open. 'The man's waiting. You can make your calls later. There are phones where we're going.'

Raven scribbled a note to Kirstie and propped it against her picture. He took his trenchcoat and umbrella.

'OK, let's go,' he said.

Baptiste drove east along the Embankment. Raven kept an eye on the rear-view mirror, thinking of Sheffield. Baptiste swung the car left after Blackfriars Bridge, negotiated a network of one-way streets and stopped in front of a grey stone building. A uniformed doorman hurried out with a golf umbrella. Baptiste gave him the car keys. Raven followed Baptiste across the chequered marble flooring to a row of lifts. The end one bore a sign. PENT-HOUSE ONLY.

Baptiste opened the gate. The interior was padded with burgundy leather and smelled of scent. The lift rose soundlessly. The two men stepped out into an empty waiting room decorated tastefully with Habitat furniture and some Impressionist prints. There was a telephone on the table, magazines.

Baptiste straightened his tie. 'Make your call,' he said,

nodding down at the telephone. 'I won't be long.' The door closed behind him.

The telephone was disguised as a musical box. Raven ignored it. This was no time to take chances. A photo-portrait by Karsh of Ottawa dominated the view from the lift. The sitter was a bald-headed man in his sixties with an undershot jaw and belligerent stare. It was George Brewster's favourite picture and used much in his many newspapers. The Man with the Common Touch. The People's Champion.

Of course, thought Raven. It had to be someone like that, someone with both the means and the motivation.

Baptiste pushed his head round the edge of the door. 'He'll see you now.'

He tapped on the neighbouring door and vanished. French windows opened on to a sodden roof garden. The man behind the Georgian desk was older and fatter than his likeness. Skilful tailoring concealed the flab on his body. There was nothing that could be done for his jowls. His voice seemed to come through a gravelbed.

'Sit down,' he invited, gesturing with a small gold figure of a goat. Its eyes were fashioned from topaz. 'You know who I am, of course?'

'Who doesn't?' said Raven.

Brewster pursed his full lips as though he had been paid a compliment. 'You don't seem surprised.'

'I'm getting too old for that,' said Raven. 'Baptiste said you wanted to talk business. I'm here to listen.'

Brewster positioned the goat in front of him, the animal stretching for something beyond its reach.

Phlegm troubled Brewster's diction. He cleared his throat.

'There are no listening devices in here, no nonsense of that sort. We can talk frankly and freely. You're not a rich man, Mister Raven?'

'No,' Raven admitted. He grinned. 'I have been close on a couple of occasions.'

Brewster's jowls quivered as though he had been told

a dubious joke. 'That's what confuses me. These people you mix with, the Greeks and the Arabs. Why haven't you gone to them for help?'

Raven's reply came readily. 'They're in a different sort of business. They don't invest in things that they don't understand. Added to which I've had some unpleasant experiences with them. I had to consider my well-being.'

Brewster swivelled his chair to face the windows. 'You know, you remind me of the chap who comes late to a poker game. Everyone's just about to go home. But the man sits in and draws a good hand. He bets it and clears the kitty. It isn't the sort of thing that makes people popular.'

'It's got nothing to do with popularity,' Raven said. 'I'm talking about survival.'

'You're a bold man,' said Brewster. 'I can see why you've been successful. Have you any idea what you're supposed to be buying?'

'No,' said Raven. 'But then nor do you. All you know is what Dunbar told you. You've already lost a great deal of money, but you still want to dabble. That's good enough for me.'

Brewster digested the answer. 'How much money do they want?'

'The price has gone up,' said Raven. 'They want a cashier's cheque for a million dollars US. They won't bargain. It's either that or nothing.'

Brewster swivelled his chair back to its original position. 'How much time have they given you?'

'I've got another four days,' said Raven. 'If I don't agree to their terms, they'll take the offer somewhere else.'

'And the codes?'

'That's been agreed,' said Raven. 'They've promised to put a picture up on the screen. If I like what I see I buy it.'

Brewster was giving every response his full attention, his eyes fixed on Raven's face.

156

'What are you looking to get out of it, Mister Raven?'

Raven knew that this was going to be important. 'Ten per cent. Ten per cent on any business we do together. Including the rest of the discs on offer. I'm not asking for anything up front. Just the money to deal with. I'll take your word for the rest.'

Brewster pursed his lips and nodded. 'I like your style. I've written off Dunbar's half million. I can afford it. But I'm a businessman, not a charity. I don't like losing money. That's why I'm going to take a chance on you. I'm not in the habit of making threats, Mister Raven. I rarely find that it's necessary. But there's something you ought to know. If you do decide to take off with my money, you may not be dead but you might as well be. I shall make it my business to find you.'

'I've been around a long time,' said Raven. 'I know the rules.'

Brewster struggled to bring his face close to the voice-box. 'Anastasia? Will you ask Mister Patel to step in for a moment?'

He scribbled a note on a piece of bond paper. 'An honest accountant,' he said. 'I doubt it'll last long. The world is full of deception, my friend.'

'Amen,' said Raven.

Someone tapped on the door. A middle-aged Hindu came in, bespectacled and deferential.

'Yes, Mister Brewster?'

'I want you to call Mister Luar at Amibank. Tell him to prepare a cashier's cheque for a million US dollars. Tell him to do it now. Take a cab there and back and bring me the cheque. OK?' He gave the accountant the written authority.

The door closed again.

'When do you think you'll be back?' asked Brewster.

Raven lifted a shoulder. 'Three or four days if I leave tomorrow. I'm expected.'

'Good,' said Brewster. 'Don't send messages or phone

157

calls. The next time we meet I want to see the goods in your hands. I'll be waiting.'

'Fair enough,' said Raven. 'Just as long as you don't forget our bargain.'

'I don't forget,' Brewster said heavily. He seemed to lose interest suddenly. He leaned over the voice-box again. 'Anastasia? Bring in the letters.'

A tall dark girl with a willowy body placed some typewritten sheets in front of Brewster. She nibbled a lip, averting her gaze from Raven as Brewster went through each thoroughly. Brewster examined a pile of telex messages, making notes on some, throwing others into the wastepaper basket. 'Thank you,' he said pleasantly.

Brewster moved to the window. He remained there until the accountant came into the room again, the cashier's cheque in his fingers.

Brewster inspected it. He handed the cheque to Raven. 'There's no need for a receipt,' he said pleasantly. 'Goodbye, sir, I look forward to seeing you again soon.'

Raven put the cheque in his wallet. 'Goodbye, Mister Brewster.'

Raven was left to make his own way down to the lobby. He opened his umbrella and ran for the nearest payphone. He got Sheffield on the emergency number.

'We cracked it!' said Raven. 'I've got the cheque in my pocket. Do you know who it was?'

'George Brewster,' said Sheffield. 'He's been on my shortlist ever since this thing started.'

'Can you get hold of Brodsky?' said Raven. 'Tell him we'll be on the Czech Air Lines flight to Prague in the morning.'

'He's calling me at five,' said Sheffield. 'I'll come to your place at six. OK?'

'OK,' said Raven. 'We'll see you then.'

He managed to get to his bank before closing time. He withdrew the five discs he had deposited and walked fifty yards to his travel agency. The girl issued his tickets.

'Prague's getting full,' she warned. 'I'm not sure I can get you into the same hotel.'

'Don't worry about it,' he said. 'We'll be staying with friends.'

He took a taxi back to the boat. Kirstie hadn't come home yet. He opened a suitcase in the guestroom and pulled out a moneybelt. It was made of elasticated fabric with three chamois pouches and a zipped container. He put the six computer discs in the pouches and undid his shirt. He fastened the moneybelt round his midriff, buttoned his shirt again and stood sideways in front of the mirror. There was no sign of a bulge. He removed the belt and carried it back to the bedroom.

He called the Prague number that Rotbart had given him. A voice answered in Czech.

'Do you speak English?' asked Raven.

'I speak,' said the voice.

'Tell Rotbart that his friend from London will be back tomorrow. His friend from London,' Raven repeated.

Chapter Eleven

The door signal buzzed like an angry hornet. Raven had drawn all the curtains. He opened the door to the deck. Rain fell in stair rods, pinging off the metal lamp-shield. Michael Sheffield appeared on the gangway looking like Cap'n Skipjack in yellow oilskins and a lifeboatman's hat covering the back of his neck. He removed the protective clothing before stepping on to the sitting-room carpet. Raven hung it over the kitchen sink to drip dry. Sheffield was sitting with his eyes closed when Raven went back. The bottoms of his trousers were still furled in bicycle clips.

Raven shook his head in wonder. 'You mean you actually *cycled* here?'

Sheffield opened one eye after the other. 'Why not? It's quicker. I'm a great believer in tactical mobility.'

Raven snorted. 'You're daft. Can I get you something to drink? You name it, there's a chance that we've got it.'

'No thanks,' said Sheffield. 'I can't stay long. I only came by to see you.'

'OK,' said Raven. 'You've seen me,' he said, poker-faced. 'Do you want to go now or will you stay to see Kirstie? She should be back any moment.'

Sheffield's gaze took in the room. It settled on Raven's prized Klee. He made no comment. Raven fixed himself a Scotch and water.

'What do you think about Brewster? The bastard never turned a hair when it came to the money.' He imitated

160

Brewster's guttural delivery. ' "I want you to get a cashier's cheque for a million United States dollars. And bring it back quickly!" He could have been asking for a pound of pork sausages.'

He took the cheque from his wallet and gave it to Sheffield.

Sheffield stirred himself, holding the cheque to the light and feeling its texture. He put it back on the table between them. 'I just talked to Brodsky. He said to tell you he'll be at the airport to meet you. Don't worry about a hotel.'

'And that's it?' asked Raven. 'Didn't he say anything else?'

Sheffield offered his tight-lipped smile. 'I've never known Brodsky to show any excitement, but this time he was speechless. He thinks you did splendidly. I agreed.'

'Brewster gave me a warning. If I lost his money he'd know where to find me.'

'Fuck him,' said Sheffield. 'The man with the friends in high places, the man they can't muzzle. I'm going to get a lot of pleasure putting the spotlight on some of his activities.'

He was on his feet before Raven as the sitting-room door opened.

Kirstie came in, wriggling out of her Burberry. Raven made the introductions. Sheffield bowed. 'I've heard a lot about you, Mrs Raven.'

She threw her bag on the couch and sat down next to Sheffield. 'If you're talking about my husband,' she said composedly, 'I happen to be in his good books at the moment.'

'Not him,' said Sheffield. 'Brodsky. He's looking forward to seeing you again tomorrow morning.'

She swung her head sideways at Raven. 'Is this true, John?'

'Yep,' he said briefly.

She took the cashier's cheque in her fingers. Like Sheffield she looked at it closely.

161

She turned from her husband to Sheffield. 'You mean I could just walk into any old bank and ask for a million dollars?'

'They might ask you to show your driving licence,' Sheffield said gravely. 'Other than that you shouldn't have any trouble.'

She put the cheque down reverently and rounded her mouth. 'Wow!'

'Your husband pulled off a major coup this afternoon.'

'That's right,' Raven said smugly. 'She ought to be proud of me, right?'

Kirstie ruffled his hair. 'Would you like to have some supper with us, Mister Sheffield?'

He smiled regretfully. 'That's a treat I'm going to have to postpone. I've got things to do, the dog has to be fed. You know, a bachelor's dreary routine. I'm sorry.'

'Then another time,' Kirstie said.

They stood. Raven fetched the Cap'n Skipjack suit. The oilskin had shed the water. Sheffield pulled on the lower half and struggled into the jacket. He pulled the drawstring tight under the sou'wester. It left his face looking impish. He raised Kirstie's hand to his lips. 'Goodbye, Mrs Raven.'

Raven winced as he saw the look on his wife's face. It was the innocent stare that preceded one of her bombshells.

'Tell me something,' she said to Sheffield. 'I'm curious. Who do you work for, exactly?'

Sheffield showed no reaction. She might have been asking where he bought his groceries.

'I'm a civil servant,' he said. 'Sometimes it's dull, sometimes it's lively. This is one of the better times.'

They watched as he lumbered through the rain without looking back.

Raven locked and bolted the door. Kirstie was on the couch, smiling artlessly.

'That wasn't a very smart thing to do,' he disapproved.

'It wasn't meant to be smart,' she replied. 'I wanted to hear what he'd say.'

'You put him in an embarrassing position.'

'I doubt it,' she said. 'I'm sure it isn't the first time he's had to answer a question like that. I don't think Mister Sheffield is easily embarrassed. You're right about him being sure of himself. But I like him. He's a charmer.'

'He's a hard-nosed intelligence agent,' said Raven.

'That too,' she replied. 'A charming hard-nosed intelligence agent.'

'And me?' he challenged. 'What would you think that I do for a living?'

She made a lithe movement that swung her feet to the floor. She considered him.

'You? You're just a middle-aged man with itchy feet. But I'll tell you this. Sheffield admires you.'

He heard the tag end of her remark on his way to the bedroom. He came back wearing his blazer over the moneybelt. He pirouetted in front of her and opened his shirt, showing the belt round his waist.

'What do you think?'

She beat her palms softly together. 'Brilliant! For one thing it stops you slouching. But why do you have to wear it?'

He stripped off the moneybelt and put the cashier's cheque in the zipped compartment. He tapped the side of his head.

'I'm a man who has vast experience in these matters,' he said smugly. 'I'm going to be carrying a million plus. Some wastrel may think I'm a likely prospect.'

She sniffed. 'Stuff and nonsense. Brodsky will be there.'

'Sheffield didn't think it was nonsense,' said Raven.

She changed the subject immediately. 'OK, let's think about supper. How about scrambled eggs? Since the white doesn't bother you like that.'

'Scrambled eggs would be fine,' he said. He took the belt back to the bedroom.

163

They ate on their laps, in front of the television screen, talking. It was a quarter past ten when they retired. Kirstie had the radio turned low on the pillow beside her. Sinatra's voice sang about having one last drink for the road. Raven put his book down suddenly. He levered himself into an upright position, belly in, shoulders squared. He transferred his gaze from the mirror to Kirstie.

'What do you mean *slouch*? I'm six feet four, for crissakes. I can't always be standing like a drill sergeant.'

She silenced the radio and placed it on the floor beside her.

'You're a fine figure of a man,' she said. 'And I'm very proud of you, lover. Now if you want to put that light out, I'll prove it.'

The bus that was ferrying passengers from the plane stopped sideways on in front of the terminal building. Journalists waited inside, one with a camcorder. Their quarry was a Czech ballerina returning from London. The Ravens were among the first to leave the bus, carrying their coats and flight bags. Raven pushed forward doggedly, a tall figure in blazer and flannels. Kirstie followed a few paces behind in a blue shirtdress and a deep-brimmed straw hat.

Only one window was open for passport inspection. There was no sign of Brodsky. Raven and Kirstie waited their turn patiently. A frontier guard checked Raven's passport and motioned him on, then Kirstie. A customs officer waved them through the green channel. Tall screens herded them into the Arrival Hall. A few people were hanging over the barriers shouting recognition. Children scampered past men holding up boards touting for hotels and car rental firms.

Kirstie was the first to see Brodsky. She grabbed at her husband's arm.

'Over there!' she said, pointing. She started to run

164

towards the exit, hampered by the tightness of her dress. Brodsky came to meet them, an arm for them both.

'Irena's waiting outside,' he said. He was wearing his green velvet suit and cardigan. Dark hair sprouted in the neck of his open collar. He hurried them out into the wan spring sunshine. A small Mercedes pulled out in front of the waiting taxis and braked to a halt in front of them. Irena was driving.

Brodsky opened the front passenger door for Kirstie and got in beside Raven in the back.

Irena looked in the rear-view mirror and smiled at Raven. 'Welcome back, John!' Her elegant hands were gloved and she was wearing a pale-green coat.

She drove the Mercedes along the periphery road and turned right on to the Prague freeway.

Brodsky pitched his voice above the hum of the motor. 'I want to thank you both. You've been very brave, Kirstie.'

She twisted round in her seat. 'Not me,' she said quickly. 'It's John who's the brave one.'

'You're going to have to lose him,' said Brodsky. 'For a day or so anyway.'

'That sounds like music to my ears,' she said, smiling. 'Do I still have to talk to him?'

Brodsky chortled. 'Not even that. Irena's taking you up to a lodge that her family owns in the mountains. There's a lake and deer in the forest. Like Canada. John and I will be joining you later.'

'OK,' she said. 'Take care of him. He's not much to look at but he's all I've got.'

This was a new Kirstie they were seeing. Raven wondered what the other two made of it. He looked away through the window. Some of the fields were water-logged. But the trees and bushes were verdant and spring bulbs bloomed on the sides of the highway. The Prague skyline revived all his memories. The women were prattling in front, Kirstie laughing.

Raven found himself voicing his thoughts.

'Is this what you really want?' he asked quietly. 'I mean Force Four, Sheffield and all the rest of it?'

Brodsky folded his hands in his legs and locked his thumbs together. His dark eyes seemed to grow brighter. 'No. Certainly not for the rest of my life. It's something I have to do until it's finished. You've been magnificent, John. It has helped us enormously.'

'I've been scared,' said Raven. 'There's nothing like fear as an incentive. What's the next move?'

The women in front were still talking but Brodsky lowered his voice. 'Everything has been made ready here. But you're going to bait the trap.'

'I've got the bait in my moneybelt,' said Raven. 'The cheque and the discs. What's the plan?'

'I've booked you into a small hotel near the Main Station. Some of my students used to stay there. The proprietor was in prison with me. There's no food and it can get noisy. But you won't be there for long.'

The older man's voice found an inner rhythm in Raven. 'Whatever you say,' he replied.

'It's a five-hour drive to the mountains,' said Brodsky. 'Irena will drop us off first.'

The moneybelt was chafing Raven's hips. Sweat dampened the back of his shirt. He was getting too long in the tooth for this sort of self-indulgence. But Brodsky was older. Maybe Brodsky saw things differently.

There was no more talk until the car started bumping over tramlines. Brodsky leaned forward, guiding Irena through the maze between the Main Station and the lower end of Wenceslas Square. The car stopped in a shabby side street. There were a few shops selling souvenirs and cheap luggage. Beyond that a café with a couple of tables outside. Then the Gellert Hotel. The front had been newly painted. Irena pulled to the kerb.

A hooker on an early shift left the café with a quick glance at the Mercedes. She was a tall girl, with jet-black hair, dressed in a short skirt and a silver-fox cape. She walked away in the direction of the railway station.

Kirstie turned round to Raven. 'It doesn't look as though you'll be short of company, my darling.'

'He won't have time for that.' Brodsky picked up Raven's flight bag and opened the rear door.

Kirstie took Raven's face in her hands. Her fingers were warm, her eyes full of confidence.

'I love you,' she said. 'Take good care of yourself.'

'I will,' he promised. 'Goodbye, Irena. I'll see you both later.'

The two men watched until the car turned the corner. Brodsky picked up the bag again.

'You don't have to show your passport. Just put your name and address in the register.'

A rubber plant survived in an earthenware tub in the lobby. The burn-scarred linoleum was spotlessly clean. There was no lift. A narrow staircase climbed to the upper floors. Travel posters brightened the walls.

Brodsky rang the bell on the counter. A middle-aged woman emerged from an inner room. Her face lit with pleasure as she saw Brodsky. They spoke briefly in Czech. The woman transferred her smile to Raven and pushed the hotel register at him.

'Please!'

He filled in his name and address. Brodsky took the key and opened a door on the other side of the lobby. He closed the door quietly behind them. The small room was sparsely furnished. A cheap wardrobe and chest of drawers. A single bed and two chairs. A half-open plastic screen offered a glimpse of a shower-stall and lavatory. The window overlooking the street was heavily curtained. There was a phone on the bedside table.

'You can use that,' said Brodsky. 'The calls are metered but the lines are direct.'

Raven locked the door and removed the moneybelt from his midriff. He pushed Brodsky down on one of the chairs and laid the moneybelt across Brodsky's knees.

'Take a look at that,' Raven said.

Brodsky took a quick glance at the cheque. The com-

167

puter discs were his main interest. He handled each one with the care of a jeweller, as if its secret would yield to his touch. He returned the cheque, discs and moneybelt to Raven.

'Lada Homolka died early this morning. The doctors tried hard to save her.'

'Did you manage to talk to her?' Raven asked quickly.

'She never came out of the coma, poor woman. Maybe it's just as well. She didn't have much to live for.'

'Another death,' said Raven. The thought depressed him. He peeked behind the shower curtain and nodded across at the opaque bathroom window. 'What's outside?'

'The backyard.' Brodsky watched as Raven crossed to the window overlooking the street. He parted a fold in the thick lace material. A man dressed in factory overalls was reading a newspaper at a table in front of the café.

'What's troubling you?' Brodsky asked quietly.

Raven sat on the side of the bed. 'I'm not sure. I keep thinking about Henry Grattan.'

Brodsky carried a chair to the table.

'The Dunbar girl can claim his body whenever she likes. We just received clearance.'

'How did that come about?' asked Raven.

'The Prague Criminal Police were told to drop their investigations. Salin's back at his desk in the Prefektura. I thought it a wise precaution.'

Raven nodded. 'There's something we haven't discussed. This printout that Rotbart gives me will be in Czech. Rotbart knows that I don't speak a word of the language.'

'I thought of that,' Brodsky said calmly. 'Tell him that you have to fax the printout to London to be translated. Tell him the reply won't take long. The whole thing can be done in an hour. The process is instantaneous. Rotbart will know this anyway.'

'And the clerk?' argued Raven. 'I walk into the post office with God only knows what on a piece of paper and

168

ask him to fax it to London? I go back for the answer and the police will be waiting for me.'

'Not at all,' said Brodsky. 'There are hundreds of messages being sent every day. Lists of names, balance sheets, confidential information. Forget the clerk for the moment.'

'Suppose Rotbart sticks a gun in my ear?'

Brodsky snorted. 'That's the last thing he'll do. Believe me. I know these people. You're worth far more than a million dollars to them. Remember the rest of the discs. You represent an unlimited source of money.' He placed a piece of paper on the bedside table. 'This fax number goes straight through to Sheffield. I'll tell him to expect it. Are there any more problems?'

Raven shook his head.

Brodsky pointed down at the phone. 'Call Rotbart,' he ordered.

The voice was the same as before, a clatter of crockery in the background.

Raven articulated clearly. 'This is Rotbart's friend from London.'

Rotbart was on the line immediately. 'I've been waiting. Was your trip successful?'

'Yes. I have the merchandise with me.'

'Good. Are you staying in the same place?'

'No. I'm in a small hotel near the Main Station. The Gellert Hotel.'

'A good idea,' said Rotbart. 'Now listen. There's a Metro in front of the Main Station. Be outside the Metro at six o'clock. Alone of course. And bring the merchandise with you. OK?'

'I'll be there,' said Raven. 'Six o'clock outside the Metro.'

He relinquished the phone and pointed at Brodsky's jacket pocket. 'Is that thing working again?'

Brodsky showed him the portable phone. The room had been denuded of oxygen. Brodsky lowered the

169

window a couple of inches. A metal stop prevented it going further. Raven pointed down at the moneybelt.

'Am I supposed to take this with me?'

'Everything,' said Brodsky. 'Whatever he asks to see, you show it to him. You've got nothing to lose, John. And you're in command, remember. Just be firm. No printout, no money.'

Raven strapped on the moneybelt again. His stomach rumbled. He turned his wrist. It was twenty to five, an hour later than London.

'I'm hungry,' he said. 'I haven't eaten since breakfast.'

'No problem,' said Brodsky. He struggled up from the chair. 'I have some things to do anyway. We'll go through the yard at the back.'

Raven slipped into his trenchcoat. The reception desk was empty. Brodsky opened a door to the yard. There were a couple of dustbins, some empty paint pots and a few cooped chickens. Brodsky took a key from his pocket. They emerged on an empty street.

Brodsky pointed at a tavern on the corner. 'You can eat there. The Metro's five minutes' walk away. Turn left coming out and you'll see it in front of you. I'll be in your room by the time you've finished with Rotbart. It's vital that I see the printout before you fax it to London.'

'I'll be back,' Raven promised.

Brodsky stumped off in the opposite direction.

Raven took his time with his meal, constantly watching the entrance. Nobody gave him a second glance. It was five minutes to six when he positioned himself at the top of the steps leading down to the Metro. Passengers surged from below, hurrying to make their connections. Trains rattled past, blocking Raven's view of the ornate railway station. The din was incessant. The homeward-bound rush of people jockeyed for buses and trams. Raven had no idea which direction Rotbart would come from. He bought a copy of *Time* at the newspaper stand and moved back to his original vantage point. A car horn drew his attention. A dirty-grey utility-wagon had pulled to the kerb. He could see Rotbart at the wheel. Raven pushed his way through the crowd and climbed on to the front bench.

The Skoda moved forward. Rotbart was wearing a new leather jacket and the brown stocking cap. He drove ingeniously, an eye on the rear-view mirror. He changed lanes at the last possible moment and doubled back in the same direction. The third time they passed the Main Station, Rotbart swung left on to a tree-bordered avenue. Lamp-posts shed light on a deserted football stadium, the empty benches, billboards advertising forthcoming features. Rotbart pulled in behind one of them and switched off the motor and headlamps. The glow from the dashboard lit his face. He offered his hand, his voice unexpectedly friendly.

'It's a pleasure to see you again, Mister Raven.'

'I'm tired,' said Raven. 'I'd like to get this business over as soon as possible.'

Rotbart twisted round in his seat. 'Everything's ready,' he said, indicating the two cases on the floor behind.

Raven recognised the shape of a laptop computer. The other case would contain the printer.

'Have you brought the discs with you?' asked Rotbart.

A car drove past fifty yards away.

'I keep my word,' Raven said steadily. The wrong move, the wrong sort of eye contact even, could mean disaster. He forced himself to meet Rotbart's unwinking stare. 'There's something that we have to get straight first.'

Rotbart peeled his lips from stained teeth. 'Did you bring the money or not?'

Raven placed the six discs on the seat, the cheque on top of them. Rotbart held the cheque under the light and returned it.

'We had an agreement,' he said. 'You've kept your word. I've kept mine. You can choose any of these discs that you like. I will show you the printout. I don't see the problem.'

171

'We have to talk frankly,' said Raven. 'You mentioned more discs before I went back to London. My friends are certainly interested. But they do have to know what they're buying. They want me to fax the printout to London so that they can at least be sure what they're buying.'

Rotbart's hand hovered over the computer discs. 'I've already told you. Go ahead and choose one.'

Raven pointed at random. One would be as good as another.

Rotbart picked up Raven's selection. 'Stay where you are!'

Raven watched him climb over the front seat and turn on the roof lamp. He sat on the rear seat and lifted the laptop computer. It was about a foot wide, a little less in depth and weighed seven kilos including the batteries. The bubble-printer on the floor was slightly smaller. Rotbart switched on both machines. The underside of the computer formed a screen that was lit from the back.

Rotbart checked the disc against a list he produced from his pocket. He slotted in the disc and pressed a button. A single word in Czech appeared on the screen. Rotbart looked smug. He consulted the typewritten list again, mouth moving as he punched the computer keys. The effect was instantaneous. Serried lines of data showed on the screen. The printer sped at eighty characters a second, whisper-quiet. The two pages were completed in half a minute.

Rotbart straddled the front bench and resumed his place at the wheel. He put the printout down with the discs and the cheque. 'Go on, take them,' he said.

Raven put the printout and cheque in his wallet, the discs in his trenchcoat pocket.

Rotbart's chin rose. His eyes gave nothing away. 'We're not cheats, Mister Raven.'

'I wouldn't be here if I thought you were,' answered Raven. 'I'm just obeying instructions.'

Rotbart turned the ignition key. The headlamps lit the

expanse of cinders. Traffic was building up along the avenue.

Rotbart looked sideways at Raven. 'Where are you sending the fax from?'

Raven was feeling more confident. 'The main post office. The reply won't take long. No more than the time it takes to make the translation.'

'An hour?' pressed Rotbart.

'I don't know,' said Raven. 'I'll just have to wait.'

Rotbart seemed content with the answer. 'I'll drive you there.'

Instinct told Raven to open the passenger door and keep running.

'I have to go back to the hotel,' he said. 'I've left the fax number in my room.'

'Is there a phone you can use?'

'There's one in my room.'

Rotbart engaged the gears. He glanced right and left until he saw the chance to join the line of cars. Both men were silent until the Skoda stopped in front of the hotel. The café was busy. Pop music blared. A group of girls occupied the tables outside.

Rotbart turned to Raven again. 'There's someone who wants to see you. As soon as you have your reply you must come back to your room and wait. Don't move until you hear from me.'

'I won't,' said Raven. The Skoda was gone before he reached the lobby. A man and a woman were climbing the stairs. The receptionist smiled and gave Raven his key. He opened his room. Brodsky was lying on the bed with his feet up. He pointed at the door. 'Lock it.'

Raven came back and produced his wallet. He put the printout on the bed beside Brodsky.

The Czech adjusted a pair of reading-glasses and pulled the lamp on the table closer. His face was stiff with anger when he finished reading the two sheets of paper.

'This is even worse than I thought. These people have to be stopped, John.'

Raven took Sheffield's fax number from the drawer. 'I'm still not sure about Rotbart. It was all too easy. I mean, I could be a hundred miles away by the time he makes his next move.'

Brodsky pushed the printout across the bed, his expression untroubled. 'Did he mention the rest of the discs?'

'A couple of times. He said there was someone who wanted to see me. I got the impression that the two things were linked.'

'Then that is your answer,' said Brodsky. 'It's of vital importance that you do exactly what Rotbart told you to do. Get the reply and wait for him to contact you. If you have any problems at all you know how to reach me. I won't be too far away.'

Raven felt for his passport and wallet. 'I'd better be going.'

Brodsky unlocked the door. The lobby was empty again.

'I'll go out the back way,' said Brodsky. 'You use the front. And remember, whatever you do stay calm.'

It took Raven ten minutes to walk to the main post office. People were standing at desks writing letters. Others waited to use the payphones. Raven crossed to the fax counter. A clerk was leaning over the machine, picking up incoming messages.

'Excuse me!' called Raven. 'Do you speak English?'

The clerk continued to stack the fax forms on a shelf. Only when he finished did he give Raven his attention.

'Not very well,' he smiled. 'But I understand better.' He was young, wearing a bombazine protective jacket and tinted glasses.

Raven slid the printout across the counter. Whatever Brodsky said was usually right. He gave the clerk Sheffield's fax number. The clerk placed the message on the machine in readiness. 'You have your passport, please?'

Raven felt in his blazer. The clerk copied the details into a register.

'Five hundred crowns, please.'

Raven paid him. The fax machine clattered. The clerk returned the two sheets of paper.

'I'm expecting an answer,' said Raven. 'Will you still be here in an hour?'

The clerk smiled again. 'Until six o'clock in the morning. Goodbye, sir.'

The lower end of Wenceslas Square was well lit and crowded with people. Raven recreated his first meeting with Brodsky. The seedy vaudeville theatre, the smell in the dressing room. Clearest of all was the memory of the sixty-year-old academic with his outrageous appeal to some kind of tribal loyalty, the insistence on the need for retribution.

Raven kept to the central walkway, passing the lovers huddled on benches, the teenagers skylarking in doorways, the cinemas thronged with patrons waiting to collect their tickets. Raven sat down at a table in front of the Café Mozart. He ordered a coffee from the waiter who had served him the week before. The man showed no sign of recognition. Raven's copy of *Time* was two weeks old. He put it down and observed the parade that was passing in front of him. This was a choice beat for upmarket hookers. They loitered and posed, checked the scene in their hand-mirrors. They competed for attention with hucksters and street entertainers. An elderly man with the painted face of a clown set up a horned phonograph and started to shuffle in time with the music.

Raven watched half-heartedly. It was almost half past eight when he entered the post office. The payphones were still being used. A youth in hotel livery was leaning on the fax counter. The youth collected a sheaf of messages. Raven showed the clerk his passport.

'Is there anything for me?'

The clerk searched through a pile of fax forms, ticked Raven's name on the register and pushed the form across the counter. It was addressed to Raven, care of Poste

175

Restante, Prague. There was no provenance given, no signature.

TEXT AGREED ENQUIRE ABOUT FUTURE TRANSACTIONS

Raven stuffed the fax in his trenchcoat pocket and hurried back to his hotel. There was a younger woman at the reception desk. The door to the inner office was open. She gave Raven his key without comment.

He locked the door behind him. The bedside lamp was still burning. He looked at his overnight bag, the wardrobe. Nothing had been disturbed. He lifted the telephone and heard the reassuring buzz. He took his coat off and sprawled on the bed and waited for Rotbart to call, making a fresh attempt to read his magazine. The words started to blur. The magazine dropped to the floor. Maybe he needed his eyes retested. He turned off the lamp and lay in the darkness. A car door slammed in the street outside. Music still blared. The brake eased on Raven's consciousness. His eyelids dropped. They lifted again. A shadow showed in the crack of light under his door. Someone tapped on it.

Raven grabbed his trenchcoat and tiptoed across the room. He turned the key swiftly and jerked the door open. Rotbart was standing there with a finger against his lips. The receptionist was halfway up the stairs, her back to the lobby, preceding a man and a woman. Rotbart pushed Raven towards the street. He was wearing a tie under his leather jacket.

The two men exited. The girl Raven had seen a few hours earlier had a foot up on the Skoda's front bumper. She was wearing the silver-fox cape and twenty-inch skirt, her long black hair reaching down to her shoulders. She took her foot from the bumper and smiled at Raven seductively.

'You are very handsome,' she said to Raven in English. 'I have nice room. You come with me?'

Rotbart jerked his thumb, snarling in Czech. The girl

176

held her ground until both men were in the car. Rotbart watched as she swaggered towards the café.

'You look like a tourist,' he said. 'These women want foreign currency. Did you get your reply?'

Raven displayed the fax form. Rotbart showed his teeth briefly.

'My friend will be interested. Where is your wife, Mister Raven?'

The question was totally unexpected. 'She's staying with some English friends,' Raven said easily.

Rotbart buckled his seatbelt and switched on the motor. He turned right at the first set of signals, away from the city centre. After a couple of miles, he joined the traffic over the long bridge spanning the Nusle valley. A Metro line ran under the six-lane highway. Raven looked down on the rooftops. Rotbart was showing signs of nervousness. The radio was tuned to a man's voice barking through static. Rotbart lowered the volume.

'Police,' he said. 'They are talking about an accident.'

He turned on to the next exit ramp. Sodium lamps lit the way below. Factories stretched in both directions, protected by barbed-wire fences. A television tower spiked the skyline on their left. Raven glanced behind. Nothing had followed them off the ramp. The only vehicle in sight was a container truck yards ahead, diesel fumes blowing out of its exhaust. There was no indication of the help Brodsky had promised.

Raven had a quick surge of apprehension. 'Where are you taking me?'

Rotbart gestured for silence. His ear was still glued to the police broadcast. He silenced the set after a few more seconds.

'We are going to meet my friend. Don't worry about it.'

He took the next right, a service road that led to the back of the industrial complex. The lighting was bad, just a few widely spaced lamps on poles over a waste of rusting scrap metal and empty oil drums. Rotbart drove as far as

177

he could. A dingy concrete building stood stark in the shaft of light from the headlamps. Rotbart switched off the motor, plunging the car and the building into total darkness. A guard dog barked somewhere beyond the tall fence. The sound seemed to come from another planet.

Rotbart reached behind for a bottle of whisky. The computer and printer were still on the floor.

Rotbart nodded across at the building. 'I'm going to set the computer up.'

Raven's foreboding increased. It was impossible to see more than twenty yards. Beyond that was unknown territory.

'I think I'll stay in the car,' he said.

'No,' Rotbart said firmly. 'My friend wouldn't like it.'

Raven pulled back the door-catch. 'I made the deal with you. Not your friend.'

Rotbart jerked his head at the building again. 'Don't be foolish. There's nobody there.'

Raven followed him grudgingly. The door to the building was daubed with anti-Communist slogans.

'It was a factory clubhouse,' said Rotbart, using a key on the door. He lit a naked bulb on a cord hanging down from the ceiling. The whitewashed walls were mapped with damp-stains, the floor littered with empty beer bottles and cigarette butts. Rotbart opened a door on the left.

'There are only two rooms,' he said. 'This and the one opposite.' He seemed intent on putting Raven at ease.

The room had been stripped of furniture. The floor was bare. Only some chairs and a table were left. There was a phone on the table. Raven glanced at the window. The steel shutters had a lock on them. Rotbart placed the bottle of Scotch on the table and took a couple of glasses from a sink in the corner. He put the glasses next to the Scotch.

'I'll get the stuff from the car. We're going to need the computer. My friend is bringing the rest of the discs.'

Sweat started to drip on Raven's ribcage. He looked at his watch. It was twenty to ten.

'I'm supposed to be calling London.'

'Relax,' Rotbart said easily. 'Everything's under control. We mean you no harm, Mister Raven.'

The door closed behind him. Raven heard the car being backed up closer. He tried the door. It was locked. Raven unscrewed the whisky bottle and sniffed the contents. He recapped the bottle and sank on a chair. There was nothing he could do except wait. Minutes crept by inexorably. A second car drew up outside. The hallway was loud with voices. The door opened suddenly. There were three new arrivals. One of them was talking to Rotbart, a second stood with his back to the entrance, the third was wearing the uniform of the Prague Criminal Police. He removed his cap, kicking the door shut as he came into the room. His voice was full of apology.

'I'm sorry to drag you out here, Mister Raven. My name is Miroslav Salin.'

'I don't like this,' said Raven.

'It's perfectly safe,' smiled Salin.

The two men sat down, facing one another. Salin's uniform was well cut. The buttons shone. The butt of a pistol peeped from his holster.

'Now then,' he said pleasantly, 'I understand that you have the cheque with you.'

Raven produced his wallet. Salin tucked the cheque in his tunic pocket.

'You're a man of your word, Mister Raven. It promises well for the future. I've brought more discs. You'll be able to inspect them. If you like what you see, we can negotiate.'

Raven rebuttoned his trenchcoat. 'Anything I say is subject to consultation.'

Salin scratched his chin. 'I'll need to know the name of your principal.'

Raven's gut knotted. He managed a smile. 'Come on

179

now, be reasonable. You must know that names are confidential.'

Salin's manner shed some of its charm. 'You know who I am. I have to know who I'm dealing with.'

'It doesn't work like that,' Raven said. 'These are serious people. Betraying their confidence would be tantamount to signing my own death warrant.'

Salin made a sound of contempt. 'We are Czechs, not Arabs. I have a good idea who is behind you, but I have to be sure.'

'I can't do it,' said Raven, shaking his head.

Salin's face flushed. The glasses jumped as he pounded the table. 'Then you're a fool. An errand boy. You leave me with no alternative. You have two choices. You can either go back to London empty-handed and do your explaining. Or you can give me a name and make more money than you ever dreamed of.'

He opened the door to the hallway. 'You've got five minutes to make up your mind. Don't be a loser.'

Raven sat where he was. The door was ajar. Salin was talking to Rotbart. The entrance door crashed open. The hallway filled with men dressed in dark sweaters and jeans. There was a blur of fists and weapons. Rotbart was up against the wall swinging a pickaxe shaft. Someone kicked the gun from Salin's hand. Raven joined in, struggling to wrest the pickshaft from Rotbart. A blow crumpled Raven to his knees. He staggered into the glare of a searchlight trained on the front of the building. Strong arms helped him into the back of a Mercedes. He tipped sideways, still clutching his head. A remembered voice filtered into his waning consciousness. He lowered his eyelids and slept.

Chapter Twelve

Raven opened his eyes wide. The last of the afternoon sun slanted across the red-and-gold carpet. The window was open. A recently replenished fire burned in a copper-cowled grate. He struggled up in bed, gingerly feeling behind his ear. The skin was unbroken but there was a lump on the back of his head the size of a walnut. He was clothed in an old-fashioned calico nightshirt that smelled of mothballs. His clothes had been folded and lay on a red velvet chair.

His last memory was of seeing the sprawling timber-built lodge as the Mercedes came down the road from the pass. There was a lake as black as the basalt that surrounded it. Its surface mirrored the welcoming lights. He remembered being helped from the car by Kirstie and Irena, whispering voices. Then sleep had claimed him.

He pushed himself further up in the bed, surveying the room. Portraits of people he supposed to be Irena's ancestors hung on the brocade walls. There were two brassbound military chests, more red velvet chairs. A dressing-table was decked with ivory-backed brushes and a picture of a startled-looking Irena wearing pigtails.

The door to the bathroom stood open. A pile of navy-blue towels was draped on the side of the tub. A matching towelling-robe hung from a hook. There was a pair of heel-less slippers on the floor below. His wristwatch was on the commode near the bed. It was twenty minutes to four.

He donned the robe and slippers and slopped to the

181

window. Conifers climbed towards the waning sun. The mountains were still crowned with snow. An empty helicopter with Czech Army markings squatted on the lawn beyond the cobbled driveway. The lake looked much smaller in daylight. The sound of voices rose from below.

Raven opened the bedroom door. There were two staircases, one on each side of a gallery hung with the glassy stare of animals displayed as hunting trophies. The voices grew louder as he neared the flagged hallway. He turned a handle, self-conscious at his attire, the greying stubble on his cheeks. A fire burned in a stone chimney. It was a civilised room with paintings of pastoral scenes, a profusion of books and magazines, bowls of pot pourri, a harpsichord. Irena and Brodsky were playing chess by the window. Brodsky was wearing a knickerbocker suit, brown boots and thornproof stockings. Irena's hair was piled on top of her head. A full skirt and laced bodice gave her the look of a Ruritanian noblewoman dressed for a fête.

Kirstie was sitting on a couch with a girl whose face was vaguely familiar. Like Kirstie, she wore a man's shirt outside her jeans. Kirstie was first to notice him. She hurried across and kissed him. The other girl smiled from the couch. He looked at her over his wife's shoulder, searching his memory.

The girl rose and dropped an elaborate curtsy, her long black hair veiling her face for a second. 'Judith Kopytin,' she said. Her accent changed. 'I have a nice room. You want to come with me?'

'Got it!' said Raven. 'The girl in the street!'

Brodsky chuckled from the window. 'Judith is one of our best young actresses. She's the one who fixed the homing-device on the car.'

'Shut up,' said Irena. She overturned the worn silver chesspieces one by one. 'The poor man must be starving,' she said, smiling at Raven. 'I'll make some coffee and sandwiches.'

182

'Come on,' said Kirstie, taking the other girl's arm. 'We'll show these people how to play chess.'

'She cheats,' said Raven.

'So do I,' the actress retorted. 'We'll just have to see who cheats the better.'

Brodsky threw an apple branch on the fire. Sparks coruscated in the blackened chimney. He sat on the couch with Raven.

'How do you feel, John?' he asked quietly.

Raven glanced up from his borrowed slippers. 'How do you expect me to answer a question like that!'

'Politely,' snapped Kirstie. 'These two people hitched a ride from the Army especially to see you.'

Raven nodded. 'I'm sorry. The truth is I don't *know* how I feel. Bewildered, I guess. I'll be grateful when I know what the hell I've been doing.'

Irena came into the room and placed a tray on a table beside Raven. 'You will let this man eat before you give one of your lectures,' she told Brodsky severely.

'And you will be quiet and mind your own business,' Brodsky said smiling.

The sandwiches on the tray were cold roast beef garnished with gherkins. One was enough to curb Raven's appetite. He put his coffee cup down. His cigarettes were up in his bedroom. There were things he had to know.

'Can I ask you a question?' he said to Brodsky.

Brodsky's magisterial head tilted. 'Fire away,' he invited.

Raven drew a deep breath. 'No bullshit. I need the truth. What was in that printout I sent to London?'

The room fell silent. Kirstie and Judith suspended their game. Irena watched from the fireplace.

Brodsky's eyes were steady. 'It was the file on Karel Novotny, a judge who resigned his post rather than put up with Communist interference. A traditionalist. A man who had the respect of all decent-thinking people. He put a bullet through his brain six months ago. The reason

183

shows on his file. He was an StB spy throughout all his student years.'

Raven filled his coffee cup. 'What about the rest of the discs?'

'They were in Salin's car. We found the codes in his pocket. They're being processed now. There are thousands of files. Men and women still in positions of trust. People in government, doctors and teachers, factory workers. All with a secret to hide. Dishonesty, sexual deviance, misdeeds committed in the heat of the moment. Salin made his choice very carefully.'

A Siamese cat jumped off the windowsill and wreathed its way on to Irena's lap. The older man's calm, reasoned voice had Raven under his spell again.

'And what have you done with Salin?'

Brodsky's jaw muscles hardened. 'He's still talking. These people have no scruples. Have you any idea what this could have meant, John?'

Raven felt gutted. 'Did Dunbar know this?'

Brodsky clasped his hands on his belly. 'Possibly. But he never had the opportunity to be certain. Brewster's another matter. His mind seems to have been on secret arms deals. Explosives supplied to the IRA and Gaddafi. He's not too particular.'

'Blackmail in other words,' Raven said bitterly. 'And this bastard's going to walk free?'

Brodsky shook his great head. 'He may have the law on his side, but he will pay, I assure you. People like Brewster need friends in high places. He's about to find out that Sheffield has severed his lifeline.'

Irena spoke from the fireplace. 'You're wasting time, Teodor. Tell him about the money.'

Brodsky's smile widened. 'The cheque has been confiscated. The proceeds will be donated to our orphanages. There's no reason why Dunbar's daughter shouldn't keep the money in Zurich. The girl is entirely blameless.'

Raven had a tinge of regret, a feeling that something he had made had been snatched away from him.

He shrugged. 'Well, that seems to wrap it up.'

The three women watched intently as Brodsky placed a small flat box on Raven's knees.

'Vaclar asked me to give you this,' he said quietly.

Raven lifted the lid. The bronze key inside was engraved with the Prague municipal arms, Raven's name underneath. He read the handwritten note that accompanied it.

Prague Castle
April 18

Greetings!

What you have done for my country transcends even friendship. Our hearts beat with yours for ever.

God bless you!

Vaclar Havel, President.

Brodsky's face creased indulgently. 'He's a writer, remember, another romantic. He wanted to give you a medal. We decided it might be an embarrassment.'

Raven put the box on the couch. The back of his neck was beginning to redden. Kirstie was on her feet, squeaking. 'We want to *see*, John!'

She snatched the box and displayed the contents to the other two women. She spun on her heel, smiling through tears.

'God dammit, I love you, John Raven! You're the best man I've ever known.'

'I just may have to remind you of that,' Raven said. 'It could be my halo that's blinding you.'

She took both his ears and shook his head gently, looking deep in his eyes.

'I see what I see,' she said fondly.

'And that's what you've got,' said Raven.

Everyone had the right to a moment like this. It was the times in between that were difficult.